I0529719

www.pagebacon.com

SMASH THE COSMOS

Short Stories of Science Fiction and Speculation

RON SACDALAN

Cover art by Jett Lascurettes

ISBN-10: 0-9964147-9-7
ISBN-13: 978-0-9964147-9-1

For Tracy

inside

DARK SUN

A pocket drone flies past the squad of soldiers, analyzing the route before them. Unseen beams of data penetrate city structures identifying threats and projecting information onto the soldiers' Head-Up-Displays as they follow on foot, viewing their environment with the highlighted sense of augmented reality. If it's green, it's clean. If it's red, it's dead. There aren't enough colors in the spectrum to represent the possibilities in between.

The soldiers jog forward, crouching low, hugging the walls of buildings. They sweep their weapons, pivoting as corners near and scanning the ledges of rooftops, ready to unleash a thousand rounds per minute on any unlucky bastard dumb enough to peak outside.

Lieutenant Calley's HUD flashes the red outline of baddies-with-big-guns when a whiz of bullets cracks heavy against the concrete wall above him.

The soldiers open-up, concentrating fire on a single position just two blocks away and five stories up. The top corner of the low-rise complex melts away in a cloud of dust and sparks, pouring rubble and bodies to the sidewalk below. The soldiers' displays go green—electronic speak for, "Stop shooting. Move forward."

They press on, following a virtual blue path that guides them down the city streets, optimizing their route for the safest passage to the biggest kill. The spheroid probe above them darts ahead, banking hard right between spiral glass towers of the city's financial center. The soldiers form a single line, hurrying past the false protection of thirty foot windows and back-to-school-displays, checking their weapons in the brief lull before the immanent next contact.

Lt. Calleys' display leads into a building one hundred yards ahead and nine floors up. Red lines trace the structure like a hell-wrought schematic diagram. He gestures to the others. "Check your systems."

A sergeant sides next to him, peering through the dark tint of Lt. Calley's protective visor. "That building's hot, sir."

Lt. Calley flips a mental coin. "*Bluebeard* says we go. We go."

"Right." The sergeant looks back and waves the men forward. "Move in."

The squad shuffles past as Lt. Calley re-checks his display: *Blue line up to ninth floor; building etched in red.*

He readies his gun and thinks, "Fuck it," following the others inside.

***

A little girl wakes to the far away sounds of artillery emanating from somewhere across the city. She isn't scared. She smiles, throwing off her blanket and rushes to draw the curtains open. She wipes the moisture from the glass with a fragile hand and dries it on the length of her sleeping gown. The rim of the horizon is aglow with the fractal dance of plasma rounds detonating behind the clouds. Her window vibrates from the fading concussive waves. A menagerie of color illuminates the night sky. She marvels at the display, teaming with wondrous thoughts. Six years old and she's never seen the sky look so pretty. She rests her elbows on the sill and her chin within her palms and whispers, "Beautiful."

She opens the bedroom door to see her father hurry past and into the kitchen of their modest two-room apartment. "Can you hear it, Papa?" she asks, following behind, a grin stretched across her face.

He rummages through the cupboards, tossing food she'd never cared for into a large duffle bag on the table. His mini-phone blinks on the counter, a message being ignored.

"Can you hear the fireworks?!"

He looks back, startled to see her. His eyes are bloodshot, his features tired. His daughter waits, delighted and anxious, rubbing her arms to fight the cold. He imagines this to be the last smile he will ever see from her. He turns away, continuing to grab at food atop the shelves, his eyes awash with tears.

"Those aren't fireworks, Elsa."

A police vehicle flies past the bedroom's fourth floor window—then another—then more. Elsa turns at a run, her eyes wide with excitement, the room strobing with red and blue light.

"No!" her father yells. "Stay away from the windows!"

She freezes in obedience as he rushes by, slamming the window shut and pulling in the curtains in one quick motion. He looks at her; still and confused. He has never raised his voice to her. She has always been a good girl.

"Is it the Sphere?" she asks, her eyes widening.

He places his hands on her arms for comfort, but she finds his tempo alarming. She can see his cheeks are damp from crying. She must have done something bad, but she can't imagine what.

"No, sweetheart. It's not the Sphere."

He sees a growing fright in Elsa and smiles, caressing her arms and taking her hands in his. "I need you to put on your best coat and walking shoes. We have to leave." He lets her go and eyes the room, pulling a satchel from beneath the bed.

"Leave?" She watches as he tosses her clothing from the drawers and stuffs them into the bag. "Why?"

The steady drone of battle steals their attention. They can feel the floor beneath them trembling in subtle waves. All the dangers of a distant world are surely at their doorstep.

"Please, Elsa. Put on your coat and shoes, and do it now."

***

An explosion rocks the building. Lt. Calley looks up to see fixtures on the ceiling shaking loose, the plaster crumbling down in heavy chunks. His Heads-Up-Display works overtime, projecting visual cues of danger he's already acutely aware of. He turns to flee and the floor collapses beneath his feet. He grabs at air. Caught in free-fall, the tonnage of concrete around him seems weightless like foam props of a vintage movie set. Down he goes in a perilous drop, from the ninth floor to the fifth.

Somewhere in the distance the pulsing thump of an energy cannon lets loose its fury on some unfortunate souls, turning solids into vapor and people into stats. Men with guns yell orders to comrades, and those without scream for mercy or run. The electricity of battle sticks in the air and straightens out your natural curls.

By some incredible luck, Lt. Calley is alive. He blinks a few times to clear his eyes, seeing nothing but darkness through dust. He can move his fingers, but can't sit up for lack of room and can only assume he's lying on his back. Concrete and rebar make for a sturdy coffin. He can't feel his toes moving—maybe they are, maybe they aren't. There's no space to move his legs even if he could. The helmet's HUD ceased to project information, with not so much as a blinking red "Farewell, Lieutenant Calley". He imagines telling this story years from now, responding, "What's the hairiest situation I've ever been in? Well, that'd be the time a building collapsed on me and crushed my legs." That's a story he'd be happy to tell some day, spinning donuts in his top-of-the-line, energy efficient wheelchair. But for now, the rest of his life seems only moments away.

Tanks roll past, shaking the earth beneath their tracks. A heavy gun fires a ball of liquid energy that sounds like an elephant being stepped on by a dinosaur being blown-up by a meteor. Whatever was in its path is probably no longer there. Small-arms spew metals just added to the periodic table and drones keep a watchful eye, recording every detail for tomorrow's situation room analysis. The only thing that hasn't changed in a billion years is the sound of *anything* impacting flesh.

Lt. Calley realizes he hasn't felt any pain up till now and when the adrenaline wears off he'll be looking at a world of hurt.

***

A civil control vehicle moves steadily forward, hovering just below the rooftops. A voice from inside booms over the public-address system, repeating warnings to stay indoors and return to homes. The defending force, it says, needs room to maneuver. "We cannot guarantee your safety," echoes down the avenues.

Far below, Elsa's tiny legs struggle to keep up with her father. The street lamps blink out in sequence, down every lane throughout the city.

People scurry en-masse, fleeing the encroaching din of weapons and machinery. Those who stay board their windows with whatever can be found. Armored vehicles cruise by overhead, their A-Grav engines rippling the air in concentric waves.

Elsa pulls her hand from her father's and stops. "Where are we going, Papa? I'm tired!"

He whips about, his momentum having flung him several paces ahead. He hurries back and grabs her hand. A steady rush of people flow past them while gunfire snaps through the crowd. "We can't stop, Elsa!"

He tugs at her, but she plants her feet. An explosion shakes the ground, freezing the crowd with fear. Pulse cannons erupt from above and the mass becomes a river. Elsa is knocked to the pavement, her father picking her up and rejoining the panicked fray. He runs with Elsa in his arms, pushing past those too scared to move and those too hurt to continue. A vehicle falls from the sky ahead and careens through a blanket of onlookers with no room to turn. The crowd shifts as one, snaking past obstacles of fire and smoke, over faceless numbers beneath their feet and soldiers running wild-eyed to meet their fate.

Elsa is too confused to scream, absorbing the horrified faces of those around her as she holds fast to her father, arms wrapped tightly around his neck, carried backwards in his arms. "Don't be afraid, my love," he says, struggling to run with bags and child. Screams erupt behind them.

They tumble to the ground. Lighting rounds of machinegun fire pepper the crowd and push it past a panic. The distinct mirage of A-Grav engines curve the air and leave it cold. The magnetic wake makes Elsa's hair stand on end. She lifts her head, her scalp moistened with sweat and thickened with blood. Her father lies like laundry in the distance, motionless beneath the pressing heels of those too scared to notice and those encouraged by bullets to run.

***

The stars can be seen through a narrow fissure between the broken concrete slabs and steel girders that pin Lt. Calley down, lying somewhere between the fourth floor and the fifth. The rubble against his back jabs at him and keeps him from trying to struggle. He steadies his breathing, steeling himself against the pain of a crushed left leg. He's certain it's bleeding but he's unable to lift his head enough to peer down past his chest. His helmet obstructs his movement, boxed in on all sides by heavy debris. Blindly, he clears chunks of concrete from his torso, moving slowly to avoid worsening his precarious situation; the rubble still seems to be settling, threatening to end his days if the bleeding doesn't end them first. Each motion of his hand loosens tiny bits of building that sprinkle on top of him, diminishing his sight and stifling his breathing. He imagines being buried by pixies with tiny golden shovels. It's cold, but sweat is filling his ears. If only he could lift his visor.

He glides his fingers over his utility belt, feeling for a familiar contour under the dust. He scrapes the dirt from the creases and blindly flips open a small compartment, revealing a button just beneath his fingertips.

With a press, a beep sounds and a red light blinks at a continuous interval giving Lt. Calley a snapshot glimpse of his predicament in-between two seconds of terminal darkness. His situation is dire. Trapped beneath tons of steel and concrete, this innocuous tracking device his only hope. He considers the odds of bleeding out before a search drone can pick up his signal. And how many others of superior rank will fall tonight and call for help within the felled remains of city spires? There could be hundreds by now and the battle just begun. Drones are sent for generals and diplomats or sinking ships with all hands down, but lieutenants and their lost platoons are far from care and never found.

"Jesus," he says aloud. A coughing fit ensues, the dust disturbed from within his lungs. *What about my men?* The pain in his chest is dreadful, his lungs at odds with air. He tries to yell out but can't. The sensation of a hammer pounds his chest. He remembers his men were on the lower floors when the bomb went off. He remembers a shout, then a moment of scuffling boots. What of them? *They must need my help.* The red light of his tracking device continues to blink every two seconds. *What does it matter?*, he relents. They are probably already dead.

Close by, he hears the unmistakable sound of a little girl crying.

***

The city burns in the distance, its orange flames illuminating the sky like an artificial sunrise. Refugees bleed from the suburbs and blanket the hills by the millions seeking asylum from an enemy they never sought to fight and were once considered kin. Their movement becomes coordinated, an innumerable band of single mind, converging in a valley below the stars and far enough away to feel the din of battle fade behind the rolling contours of the land.

They huddle close, encamped beneath a massive floating orb that seems to block out half the sky. Two miles wide and two miles up it levitates without a sound, reflecting all the eyes can see, offering the illusion of a world within this world. Nearly a dozen years since first it came to settle here from unknown parts beyond the stars; a citadel, a question mark, a source of strife and wonder.

***

Elsa sits bunched in the corner, both arms wrapped around her knees. She wipes away her tears with the sleeve of her heavy coat and looks up, past where a concrete wall was just hours before. She hasn't yet noticed her father's blood on her favorite walking shoes. She clears her eyes again and contemplates the stars as only a child can see them; decorative twinkling bulbs, just beyond her fingertips.

Her stomach growls, reminding her she hasn't eaten since yesterday and that her father's bag was taken by strangers. A tank rolls past outside shaking loose the rubble. The building across the street is on fire. She climbs further up the broken remains, hiding in the safety of the shadows.

The smell of burning synthetics irritates her nose. She can feel the residual violence of shells exploding in the distance, the shattered structure around her shaking and shifting with every closing impact. Men run past outside shooting their weapons at targets that zip by above. Bullets stray near, ricocheting around her head, bouncing off metal and chipping concrete into dust. She pulls her coat over her head and muffles a scream. If they find me, they'll hurt me. She waits for the shooting to stop then edges further back into the darkness.

Across the room she can see the faint blink of a red light from beneath a pile of broken concrete, flashing every two seconds like the message beep of her father's mini-phone.

***

Lt. Calley hears the curious steps of tiny feet climbing onto the fallen walls that surround him.

"Hello?" he calls out in a coarse whisper, careful not to scare her off. He shortens his breath, the debris loosening with each perceived foothold. Broken fragments of rock tumble down within earshot. He tunes out the muted noise of artillery and nervously rubs his fingers against his sides. He stares intently through the narrow fissure before him. Stars twinkle in the chilled night sky.

"Hello?" responds the tender voice of a little girl.

A glimpse of eyes ... then an ear ... and then a wisp of hair.

***

Three men in civilian clothes run down the thoroughfare, the rapid bolts of pulse rifles flash past them from behind. They fire their weapons blindly to the rear, skirting the buildings and keeping pace, retreating from the soldiers moving in from down the way. A drone zips by overhead and they blast it out of the sky.

A soldier's bullet finds its mark, and now the men are two.

"This way!" one shouts, leading the other between the spiral glass towers of the financial district.

***

Lt. Calley hears the heavy stomp of boots entering quickly from the street below. He covers the blinking red light of his tracking device with his hand. The footsteps move through the rubble on the lower floors, shifting the ground beneath them. He imagines them stepping on the bodies of his fallen men.

He hears the girl jump down and scurry to some unseen place.

He sighs and clenches his teeth.

"Up there," one directs, his voice deep but young. He sounds no more than twenty-five. A trickle of dislodged debris indicates they're climbing closer, making their way up a broken staircase. They move about the building, stopping then proceeding; their actions indiscernible to Lt. Calley's ear.

"Did you set the charges?" he hears the same man ask.

"Yup," the other starts, with a distinctively older voice. "If they come up here ..." he continues, presumably finishing with a gesture of assured destruction.

"Are you ok with this?"

"Would it make a difference?"

Their footsteps move closer, seemingly within the same room.

Where's the little girl? Lt. Calley wonders, hearing only the footfalls and voices of men.

"Get down!" one urges in a loud whisper, his voice indistinguishable from the other. The building begins to quake. The debris that traps Lt. Calley shakes and threatens to collapse and crush him. The menacing rumble of a heavy tank presses near followed by the dark electric hum of its turret swiveling slowly to the side.

***

Elsa puts her hands over her mouth to keep from screaming, still and unseen, waiting from the shadows as a tank rolls by outside. Its big gun turns toward her, sweeping past in search of hidden targets. She watches the two men sit themselves unaware of her presence, nervously, their backs against the wall.

The older takes a heavy breath as the tank moves into the distance. "Jesus Christ," he whispers, wiping the dirt and sweat from his face.

The younger shows his daring with a grin and checks his weapon for ammo.

"Poor Jeffery," laments the older. He pauses to think for the first time in hours. "He never got to see his girls."

Elsa remembers her father's smile. She remembers how happy he would be to greet her after school. How he gave her anything she asked for, and how he cooked strange concoctions made from kale and unpronounceable foods. She imagines Jeffery's girls to be her own age and wonders if she might know them. *Do they go to my school?* She would certainly know them because she has so many friends. *Do they like the same games or wear the same clothes?* If she only knew their names she might find them and become like sisters. She figures they're kids, and kids are always kin. Her only certainty is that they're lost without their dad to cook them food they can't pronounce and answer all their silly questions. She notices her blood-stained shoes and wipes the tears from her eyes.

***

The younger man blows the dirt from his barrel. "His girls are safe. That's what matters now."

The older man nods, unconvinced, staring down into the gaping hole that used to be the fourth floor.

"How do you know they're safe? How do you know they made it to the Sphere?"

The younger lays his weapon across his knees, placing a hand on the other's shoulder and says, "I just know these things."

***

Elsa looks to her left at that pile of concrete and steel, not fifty feet from where the two men are sitting. To her dismay, the red light beneath the rubble has stopped blinking.

***

A pair of fighters circles the Sphere at a radius of ten miles, the closest they can come before some invisible field would disrupt their electronics. The massive orb hovers silently above the valley as it has for a dozen years, protected by a force that defies all earthly comprehension. Thousands in the encampment below observe as the fighters circle twice, then depart toward an unseen base beyond the horizon.

"Why do they even bother anymore?" one refugee asks another.

"They're just beating their chests, letting us know who's still in charge," another replies, as ten thousand campfires illuminate the Sphere from below.

***

There is no safety in the Sphere, Lt. Calley thinks, knowing that his brigade would challenge the dissenters with sticks and stones if that's what it takes. *These people*, he knows, *are delusional. We aren't the enemy, it's that thing in the sky they should be afraid of! "Benign" doesn't equate to "benevolent"*. He wants to yell out to those men and tell them that the world is not theirs to forfeit, but here he is trapped between the floors of a shattered building.

He considers his situation and works to calm himself. His leg, crushed beneath a pile of concrete and steel; his breathing, shallow and quick. The pain he ignores takes a backseat to the fear of dying young, unaccomplished and unsung. But these are not the men to call out to for help. These are the cowards who put him here and would see him to his end. He can feel the liquid warmth of his blood puddling up around his waist. He struggles to keep his wits, the life draining from his body. He thinks of the wife he never had and the family he never cared for, of the men he lost this day and the world they fought to save, imaginings of childhood friends and neighbor's pets and memories of mostly stupid things. A life that he may never lead plays center stage, a hopeless show in the darkness of this solemn crypt.

And he thinks of the girl.

She must be clever, quiet, hiding in the shadows, careful not to give herself away. She must be scared, separated from her family, lost in a city under siege. He could call out to her and tell her to run, but if these men don't stop her, their bomb certainly would. He hears nothing now but distance sounds of battle muffled by a burning urban labyrinth. He would give anything to talk to her, to comfort her and have her comfort him. He knows she must be near; smart and staying low.

He can hear the closing sounds of troops moving along the streets outside. The occasional shot of rifle fire pops and fades away, quieting the shouts of desperate men. He knows full-well his battalion is coming to finish what others have started.

Something changes. The red light of Lt. Calley's tracking device has turned to blue beneath his palm. Salvation, if luck is on his side. He knows blue means a drone has picked up his signal, ready to relay his coordinates to the nearest available squad. A ticket home, but less then whole. His troops will follow the virtual scent and paint this building red, forcing down the two dissenters to pay the toll for their sedition. They will unleash their hell upon the broken walls around him and leave it ground to dust. They are men and men deserve no less.

But what of me? Trapped inside this grave of stone, subject to the same barrage of arms to come. What of my own life? What of home and better days and friends who wait with warming fires and tender words?

His eyelids weigh heavy. He struggles to remain conscious. It doesn't matter, he concludes. Our soldiers have a job to do.

And what of the girl? If the soldiers come, with their powerful guns and single minds, her life would doubtless be in jeopardy. Trapped in the surge of weapons and men, she would never live to see her family, if her family still lives to see her. Bullets will fly and bombs will explode and she, left another lost corpse of a war she can't possibly understand. Lt. Calley considers this a moment, fighting to take in air, then slides his hand down from the blinking blue light, disabling it with the press of a finger.

***

Elsa coughs and gives herself away. The two men jump to their feet with weapons drawn.

"Who's there?!" the younger asks, peering into the shadows across the room.

She struggles to hold back another cough, her throat too dry with dust.

"Come out or we'll shoot!" the man continues, moving in with weapon ready.

Elsa emerges from the dark, tears in her eyes, holding back a crying fit that makes her body shake.

The men step past her cautiously, peering into the corner shadows, over broken desks and dangling office fixtures.

Troops can be heard running past outside.

The younger man turns and looks Elsa over, pacing a circle around her. "Where're your parents?"

She cries into her sleeve, unable to respond.

"I'm sure if she knew that ..." the older man begins, lowering his weapon and removing his finger from the trigger.

The other follows suit, strapping his rifle around his shoulder. He seems disturbed by the mucus that covers the girl's lip, her sleeve glistening like the wet crawl of a snail. "Well, she definitely can't come with—"

A device around his wrist beeps, drawing Elsa's curiosity. She stifles her crying as the man manically pushes virtual buttons on the device's display.

"They're coming. We need to get to the roof," he asserts, moving his gaze to the older man, glaring at him intensely. "The kid stays."

The older man leans down pulling his sleeve over his hand and wipes Elsa's nose dry. He takes her arms gently to comfort her.

"What's your name?" he asks.

She glances at the younger man who checks his weapon for the umpteenth time. She knows he doesn't like her and it makes her scared.

"Elsa."

The older takes a knee, careful to keep his arms at length. "Well, Elsa, I need you to stay here and wait a while, okay? Maybe a long while, until it's safe. Promise me you won't go outside, alright? Wait here until somebody nice finds you and can help you get home. Do you promise?"

She wipes her mouth with a sleeve. "Okay."

***

Lt. Calley suffers an unbearable chill, his body trembles uncontrollably. His heart pulses with the hard, slow beats that precede a man's life flashing before his eyes. He hears the footfalls of the two men making their way up the stairs, pushing open doors until the final shuts hard behind them.

Close by he hears the shuffling little shoes of the girl, followed soon by a hazy glimpse of cheeks, hair, then eyes peering down at him through the cleft in his concrete tomb.

"Hello?" she calls down with a hush.

Lt. Calley struggles to lift his hand to her, hoping for a simple touch. "Elsa," slides from his lips, too soft to pass his visor.

"Hello?" she repeats, turning her head, placing an ear to the fissure.

His fingers slide, frail and torn against the rough stone, edging up toward the faint light of the stars. The air whispers gently across his skin. He knows now, he is nearly free. A stretch of measure more, then the feel of her soft hair.

She startles at his touch, turning back to peer inside. "Are you there?" she asks, reaching down with a fragile hand. "Papa?" she cries, the jagged crevice scraping at her arm.

"Yes," he whispers, reaching her delicate fingertips.

She begins to cry at the feel of his callused skin. Her tears drip down like raindrops onto his visor, clearing away the dust.

He can see the stars behind her, dimming with the dawning sky; a faint orange glow, creeping in to arrest the night. He can feel the warmth of her breath floating down to mend his tainted soul and lift him from his mortal bonds. He can see her naïve eyes peering down toward him through darkness, wanting for her father's smile.

"Be brave, little Elsa," he says, his fingers slipping away into the deep.

***

A beastly vehicle approaches from the northern sky, whipping the air into violence; a dark green dragon with spinning blades and a deafening roar; a battle machine from a primitive age. It swoops in low, hovering just inches above the rooftop, spitting fire from its sides to the streets below.

"Get in!" the gunner calls.

The two men move in, hunched low for fear of losing their heads. The rising sun casts their shadows from the east. They climb into the mechanical behemoth, worried and disheveled. It's impossible to imagine a contraption like this could ever fly. The older man looks back from where he came to find Elsa standing in the sunlight, her hair blowing wildly in the wash of the rotor blades. She lingers, staring not at the terrifying machine before her, but at the morning sky to the west. The men follow her gaze with theirs, beyond the city towers and past the rolling hills.

The great Sphere looks like a second sun, low on the horizon, reflecting the early light. They've seen this sight a thousand times, but like the sun itself, it never fails to impress. But today brings something new that seizes their attention. The great Sphere, it seems, is rising.

The hot liquid rounds of a plasma cannon breaks their attention. Elsa screams, covering her head with her coat and dropping to her knees. The helicopter wavers and rolls, the men inside holding fast to any solid fixture.

An assault vehicle nears, gliding between the buildings, letting loose a shower of molten rounds.

"Elsa!" the older man shouts, reaching out to her from the open door as glowing plasma shots whiz between them.

She jumps to a run toward the beckoning safety of the hovering green beast, listing and pulling as lightning-fast rounds impact its frame. She cries out with fright, arms extended, hoping to be caught.

A bomb explodes two floors below her, its concussive force lifting her off her feet. She lands hard, face down, her tiny hands breaking her fall. The rooftop cracks and threatens to collapse.

The helicopter swivels. The gunner fires furiously at the armored craft. The fifty-caliber rounds bounce harmlessly off its plating.

"We're leaving!" the pilot shouts, pushing hard against the throttle, lifting the dragon into the sky.

Elsa cries, pushing up from the ground, watching as her saviors abandon her. The helicopter pivots toward the north, rising above the spires. Black smoke trails behind it. Plasma rounds chase it down. It spins and rolls then drops behind city the skyline.

The armored craft, with its concentric humming waves, turns toward Elsa, hovering a hundred feet away. She can see the men inside looking at her from behind their windshield. They seem unsure of what to make of her; a little girl standing there on the rooftop, staring back at them defiantly.

But Elsa is too scared to move and too tired to cry.

The craft moves toward her slowly, distorting the sky around it. A soldier inside fiddles with controls.

"Hey kid," he says, his voice blaring over a public-address system. "Stay right there."

His voice alarms her, snapping her out of a trance. She steps back as the vehicle approaches, agitating the soldier inside.

"Don't go back inside, it's too dangerous. That building is falling apart. Hold tight and we'll send a hover to pick you up."

She turns again to the Sphere far in the distance, now much higher in the sky. Its reflective surface fades, like an inkblot against the blue horizon. Wisps of cloud seem to be drawn to it, coalescing around its perimeter like the rings of Saturn. The sky behind it seems to bend.

"Holy shit!" blares over the public-address system of the armored craft.

It lists back and down, struggling to keep control. It slides across the air, wobbling and turning, landing hard but intact on a rooftop across the way.

Elsa watches as the two soldiers climb out, the vehicle teetering from the building's side. They brush themselves off and turn their attention to the great sphere above the hills. They make their way to the western ledge, curious as children, standing together without a word to pass between them.

She gazes at this new black dot in the distance with its wondrous and terrifying possibilities, sucking in the sky around it. She thinks of dolls and rainbows and flowers and all the things she loves. Everything nice has colors. She sees nothing new but a big black hole and shrugs, her attention quickly waning. *It's not very pretty*, she thinks, wiping her hands against her sides. Her stomach growls. She scratches at an itch on her leg. She looks around and realizes the city is quiet. She slips off her shoes and wiggles her toes, feeling a cool relief. She removes her heavy coat and sits, looking over a ruined city, appreciating the warmth of the morning sun.

THE BOAT

The science vessel *Adeline* rises and falls on the ocean swells like a toy. She pitches hard to one side as the white crest of a wave lands heavy on her deck, sweeping two of her crew to the rails. They hold on for love of life and for fear of a lung-full of green Pacific. Her engines cough and sputter to a halt, choked by the saltwater that leaks into her bowels through blistering seams. She goes where the seas push, twisting this way and that inside a heavy gale that threatens to turn her over with every breath.

A crewman steadies himself, holding tight to a steel drum with one hand and his jacket's vinyl hood with the other. Another wave crashes over the side, knocking him to his knees. He yells, "John! We have to radio for help!" against a blanket of wind, his voice barely audible against the gale. He pulls himself up as the *Adeline* rolls to port, the seas rising and falling beneath her rails.

"No! We can't do that!" a woman replies, inching forward across the deck, taking handholds where she can.

Water pushes hard against her boots threatening to sweep her off the side. The wind pulls at her hood, forcing her back to steady herself against a beam. She looks to the crewman and then to John who is crouched near the engine compartment, trying to pry the hatch open. She puts a firm hand on his shoulder and turns him around. "You know we can't do that! Tell him we can't do that!"

John looks about, pondering the situation. Waves wash over the deck, each greater than the last. The ocean bellows in a tumult of liquid hills, rolling beneath them like an army of giants. He looks back to the woman, her hand still gripping his shoulder.

"She's right, Alan! We have to hold on!"

"Hold on to what?!"

Alan's hood slips off his head and tugs him back against the rail. He spins around and catches hold of the only thing that isn't sliding. From across the deck, he looks directly at the woman and wipes the spray from his eyes. "Ann, we're going to die out here! We need help and we need help now!"

Ann puts her hood on and fumbles with the drawstrings, pulling them tight. Her wet hair sticks to her face in clumps. "We can make it through this! Please, Alan, just a little longer! No radio! Not yet!"

John pulls the hatch open revealing the dormant engine several steps below. A rush of water precedes him as he hurries in, flashlight in hand, illuminating the way. Ann takes a few steps down, saltwater forces past her heels.

"No!" John calls out to her. "Go up to the helm and get ready to turn it over!"

"Right!" She rushes back out, passing Alan as he steps aside, lest he be knocked to the ground by her stride. Foamy water cascades down the stairs.

The boat rolls to one side. John falls hard against the wall, his shoulder taking the brunt of the impact.

Ann makes her way up metal steps to the control deck. The boat rolls thirty degrees to the side. She hangs on, fingers sliding over the wet safety railing.

"It's no use! It's flooded!" Alan yells down to John, who struggles to take hold of a lever between the engine's intake manifold and exhaust piping.

John shines the flashlight on the engine—it's a mess of more rust than metal. Steam bursts from its casing from each splash of water that hits its hot frame. "Tell her to try it now!"

Alan hesitates for a second, then rushes up and out. He braces himself against the stairs and shouts up toward the helm where Ann stands at the ready. "Try it now!"

The starter noises in cycles forcing the pistons to move in a desperate churn. A pause, and then another disparaging go turns the engine once more, but it fails to engage. A third burst from the starter is less effective, turning slower, chopping down their hopes.

John turns back to Alan who is standing in the hatch hanging on for a word. "Get down here and turn off the bilge pump!"

"Are you crazy?" Alan screeches back, shaking his head in opposition. "That's the only thing keeping us afloat!"

"The pump is draining the battery! We need all the juice we can get! Start up the generator!"

Alan runs down, flipping a switch along the wall. An unapparent hum quiets in the midst of the storm's fury. The motor of the electric pump slows to a halt. He takes cables and attaches one end to the portable generator, the other to the main battery terminals. With a quick pull of the rip-cord the generator comes alive. Water sloshes over his boots. An initial puff of petrol smoke congests the cabin. He double-pats John on the shoulder and heads above deck, flipping the switch to get the bilge pump back on line.

Another signal to Ann and the starter initializes. The engine turns over with new vigor, but again, fails to start. The boat heaves to starboard under a heavy gust causing John to drop his flashlight into the water at his feet. He chases it down as it rolls, illuminated below the surface. It slides underwater as the boat lists, then flickers and fades leaving the compartment darkened.

John turns back to Alan, who is holding tight to the rail, half in, half out of the stairwell.

"It's no use!" Alan yells.

He climbs up the steps to the helm where Ann stands awaiting any sort of command or confirmation. She stares at Alan as his eyes wander from her to the radio transmitter on the dash.

She sidesteps toward the transmitter, blocking it from his view. "No radio. We can't."

John emerges from below, holding on to the counter as he makes his way in. "She's right," he says, turning to Ann for affirmation, then back again to Alan. "No radio. We've talked about this. You know the situation. We have to wait this out."

Saltwater drips from Alan's hair and into his eyes, burning his frustration and fear even deeper. He stands with his lids clenched tight, his jaw about to shatter his teeth. They wait for his reply as the ocean turns the boat around.

Alan opens his eyes with an imperceptible smile, gazing out the windows to the raging seas. Mother Nature, it seems, may swallow them whole. He relaxes his stance, looking at Ann and John, contemplating his response. *This is greater than my life*, he thinks. *Don't be a coward.* He calms himself with a deep breath, looking to the others with a quiet resolve amidst the furry of the South Pacific. "We need to batten down everything," Alan says with a grin, exiting down the stairs to the main deck.

John shoots a look of relief to Ann. They exchange nervous smiles and follow Alan out, onto the deck and into the storm.

JACK AND KAWASSA

It takes all his strength to level the Kalashnikov, looking down the barrel at some imagined foe projected against the sun-baked mud walls of his home. The weapon is heavy with a full magazine and the boy's fingers are barely long enough to reach the trigger. If he actually had to fire this thing it would probably do *him* more harm than anyone on the receiving end, yet he aims at the only remaining photo of his brother, hanging on the wall in a cracked wooden frame. This was his weapon, the weapon that was to make his brother a man, the weapon of his uncles, the weapon that costs less than food. His brother would be a hero by now, the boy imagines, had he not been killed last season by the government soldiers, before he could prove his worth. There are few older boys left in his village like his brother and his brother's friends who met the unnatural death of violence or simply ran away. There are few boys left to be venerated, few boys older than ten.

The boy lowers the assault rifle, the muzzle coming to rest on the dirt floor. The persistent desert grit paints the dark skin of his feet. Flies buzz around his untouched meal, ignored on a lone table made from the carvings of a distant tree. One day they will buzz around him, he thinks, and he will lack the life to swat them away. He hears the *rat-tat-tat* of gunfire in the distance.

Kawassa, he remembers his father saying. *Fetch your brother's gun and bring it to your mother.*

***

Automatic gunfire erupts. The sounds of an urban battle ripple between the clay structures that the villagers call its center. Jack reminisces about the cheeseburger that he ate in San Francisco just hours before he got on the plane. He thinks fondly of his old suede couch, how comfortable it is, and of his home on Church Street. He thinks of his girlfriend who he neglects to think of much when back in The City. He wonders why these things seem to mean so little to him until he is dropped into a place like this—like Africa or Chechnya or Hades, where death from drinking water is as likely as from a mortar round.

Bullets whiz by, the strays chipping away at the wall above his head. Jack stands, composing himself and checking his gear. Multiple cameras swing from around his neck and shoulders as he turns quickly around a corner, snapping off pictures of the fight along the way. His bulky canvas vest barely covers the Kevlar flak jacket that might not save his life someday. A Humvee races past. The gunner on the fifty-caliber fires on unseen targets ahead to soften the path.

Jack snaps off photos of a local gunman running past armed with the requisite AK-47 and protected by nothing more than Khaki shorts and the fear of God—then ducts into an alley to his left. The armed local stops, his sweat dripping from his forehead to the handkerchief that covers a face, skin darkened by countless generations of unrelenting sunshine. He is thin and his eyes are young, but he doesn't seem afraid of the mayhem that envelopes his homeland. He catches a curious glimpse of Jack who stands poised to snap a picture but waits frozen in anticipation of a bullet to the head. Shots fire out from unknown places. The local gunman lowers his rifle and runs, disappearing down the main dirt street and out of view. No one from this country is crazy enough to take pictures in a battle and the image always catches the natives off guard. Government soldiers hurry by as Jack wipes the dirt from the beard that he hasn't bothered to tend to in months.

At the far end of the alley he can see a body dangling half out of a bullet-riddle car. The civilian clothes he wears tags him as either a local insurgent or one of the untold numbers of innocent bystanders. The government troops have tidy uniforms designed to camouflage their bodies, but only seem to make them easy targets. Jack makes his way closer, adjusting the settings of his camera as he moves.

An explosion shakes the ground. The side of the nearest building cracks from the concussion. Jack, guarding his gear, recovers then continues on, taking photos as he approaches. The body ahead is lifeless and outstretched as if the man were gunned-down making a futile escape. A Soviet-era rifle lies spent at his side. The car door hangs loosely from its hinges. One leg is still in the car while the mass of his body lies exposed in the alley. What blood he once had has mixed with the dirt beneath his head to form a kind of chocolate paste.

Jack snaps photos of the sanguine mess inside. Several books lie on the passenger seat including a bloodied copy of Charlotte's Web. Jack snaps a photo. The backseat has been removed to accommodate several ten-gallon plastic containers filled with a liquid that Jack assumes is some nasty explosive concoction which may yet to see its full potential. Wires lead from the containers to somewhere beneath the front passenger seat. It would be prudent to get as far from this scene as his feet can take him, but he cringes at the alternate prospect of taking photos for Sunset Magazine.

A hand reaches up and grabs the lens, smearing it with blood. Jack jumps, examining the camera and backing himself against a wall. The resurrected body before him moans and claws blindly at the ground, more reflex than intellect. Jack wipes the lens with his sleeve then snaps off pictures in quick succession as he tries to recall the number of times someone has died in front of him. There was the first time, in Bosnia. That much he will never forget. Two others during a Russian mortar attack in Chechnya. Thailand. Militants in Philippines. A friend in California. Nine, he thinks. Enough for a baseball team. He took pictures of all of them, including California—the only roll he didn't sell. The man before him goes limp, his eyes fixed to the perfect sky above.

Guns fire nearby. Jack leans back against the building and peers out around the corner. Two local gunmen are on a rooftop across the street taking pot shots at something down the way. He checks his camera, wiping more blood from around the lens, and takes a deep breath. Rounds crack at the dirt as he scrambles, hunched over, to the next block. He makes his way, running up close to buildings, ducking as he passes by the shattered remains of windows. Again, the repetitive crack of bullets stop him cold, blinding him with fragments and dust chipped from the wall to his side. He drops to his hands and knees, crawling forward toward the limited safety of an alley just a few feet ahead. His cameras drag along the ground, dangling from the straps around his neck.

Fifty yards ahead in another alley, a trio of government soldiers carefully makes their way forward, toward Jack. They spot him and aim their weapons. Jack raises his arms, his clutter of cameras swinging in full view. The soldiers lower their weapons, chuckling. The lieutenant up front informs Jack he is lucky they didn't shoot. *Obviously.* Jack thanks him with a smile, hidden behind his camera as he snaps off pictures. They soak-in the attention.

He aims his lens at the rooftop directly above the troopers. Two local gunmen pace the rooftop searching for targets, unaware of the soldiers gathered below in the alley.

Jack looks to the car in front of him. Whatever soul that man had has since departed for another war.

He takes a breath and leans out around the corner snapping photos of the locals on the roof. The government soldiers across the way follow Jack's line of sight to a position three stories above them.

The locals turn to Jack, returning his gaze with a spattering of gun fire, ripping holes into the brick wall as Jack ducts back for safety.

The government soldiers ready grenades.

The rooftop locals yell to comrades in the distance, pointing down to Jack's location.

A trooper lobs a grenade high above his head and onto the rooftop. A second grenade follows close.

The locals lean over the ledge, firing wildly into the alley below.

The grenades detonate, sending the two rebels falling like rag-dolls at the troopers' feet.

Jack snaps photos then runs for cover through a nearby door.

***

Kawassa listens to the gunfire around him, resting against the exterior wall of his father's shop. The

Kalashnikov weighs heavy in his little hands, pulling his arms straight, stretching them, but making him strong. His knee is bloodied from a fall during the sprint to get here, but he's glad that he found his shoes before he left. He peeks in through a shattered window. The tables are set for the afternoon coffee, but no one is here. Debris litters the floors. Bullets have downed his father's favorite painting—a mountain shepherd resting in the shade— leaving cracks in the plaster that extend to the ceiling.

The front door has been kicked from the hinges. Kawassa tightens his grip on the assault rifle and walks inside, stepping carefully to avoid the mess of splintered wood.

Glass shards break beneath his sneakers as he moves through the tiny dining area of his family's restaurant. The floral embroidery of his mother's table cloths is hardly visible beneath a thick layer of dirt and debris. The door to the small Kenmore refrigerator is open in the kitchen where Kawasaa makes his way.

Soldiers have stolen the Coca Cola. He's come all this way, from his home at the east edge of the village, through the dangerous fighting on the streets, over many dead on the ground, with helicopters watching from the sky and rockets buzzing overhead, and there's not even a sugary drink to wash the dirt from inside his throat. Hopefully his mother is upstairs. She will have something good for him. His father's sister lives upstairs and he knows where she keeps the Western treats.

He makes his way to the stairs, stopping a few steps up at the sound of a grenade hitting the floor then rolling to a stop against the wall below.

***

Jack steps inside from the alley as an explosion jolts the building. He waits, hunched over. The dirt shaken from the ceiling settles lightly on top of him. He composes himself, blowing dirt from his camera and shaking the others that hang about his body. Footsteps can be heard from another room.

The walls have been decimated by gunfire. Furniture smolders. Glass lies shattered everywhere. The room is void of life but for a severed hand lying near the staircase. A few pictures are required before making his way upstairs.

A trail of blood leads down the hall. He turns the corner and through an open doorway. A woman in black dress and red hijab holds a small child in one arm. Their eyes meet Jack's, terrified. He snaps off photos with one hand, reassuring them with the other. The woman's right arm is lifeless and dripping with blood—the previous owner of a perfectly good hand.

The *click-click-click-click* of the camera seems to drown the gunfire outside. Jack continues taking photos.

A drop of blood hits his forehead, then another. He looks up. Pools of blood have formed, saturated on the ceiling in several spots, all dripping to the floor. The woman looks as if she is losing consciousness. The child clutches at her clothing.

A helicopter can be heard, distant but closing.

Jack wrenches his gaze from the ceiling and makes his way up the stairs to the roof.

He throws open the door and steps in blood. Several men lay motionless, their life draining from them in crimson puddles. Local gunmen run across distant rooftops, shouting to each other and firing their AK-47s down to the streets below. Jack crouches his way to the ledge, lies on his belly and peers over the side. Humvees barrel down the dusty street.

An attack helicopter hovers in the distance, tearing holes in nearby rooftops with its heavy guns.

On the street below, a tribal gunman takes to one knee. He hefts a rocket launcher on his shoulder and takes aim at the infernal flying machine. Lateral gunfire peppers the ground around him and he shuffles backward. Jack snaps off photos, lying on his stomach, propped up on elbows.

He rolls over, turning back to see a boy, facing away, standing a dozen feet down and holding a Kalashnikov. The boy is a local, small, practically immune to the daily horrors of war—the next generation in zealous fighters. At the center of the rooftop is the object of the boy's attention. Jack isn't sure of what he's looking at. A small sphere, ten inches in diameter, hovers inexplicably, five feet above the center of the rooftop. The sphere is a dull silver, like brushed aluminum, and perfectly motionless. It radiates in the noon-day sun.

Jack is still, perplexed. Twenty feet away the sphere just is; an anomalous object dangling from an imaginary string. The boy stands, watching, the assault rifle pulling taut his scrawny arms. He seems more curious than entranced, as Jack imagines he should be. But kids raised in war are fearless.

Gunfire breaks the moment. Jack looks back and down to the street.

The tribal gunman below steadies himself and re-aims the rocket launcher. The copter continues to unload its heavy rounds at distant targets, seemingly unaware of the gunman below preparing to take it down.

The boy on the roof turns back, startled to see a foreigner lying on his stomach taking photos of the fighting below. He walks toward him slowly, raising the muzzle of his brother's assault rifle.

Shots kick up dirt around the gunman on the street as he peers through the sight of the rocket launcher. He closes an eye and fixes the crosshairs on the engine compartment of the helicopter which continues to unleash is cannons on targets up the way.

The boy aims his rifle at the foreigner, struggling to keep it level.

Jack turns around, still lying, catching the boy's gaze and the metallic orb that hovers silently behind his shoulder. The boy yells something in his local language that Jack can't speak, but easily understands. The boy pulls the trigger. Jack flinches, holding his breath. The boy steps back, examining the weapon, perplexed and a little embarrassed. *Please wait, while I figure out what's wrong with my fucking gun. Thank you.* It's obvious to Jack that the boy has never been shown how to load the chamber.

The gunman on the street takes a breath, holding his aim on the engine of the chopper. He pulls the trigger as a well-aimed bullet pierces his chest and knocks him back, sending the rocket buzzing off-course and into the room two floors below Jack. The explosion rocks the building and buckles the roof. The silver orb hovers motionless, unaffected. The boy is somehow still standing, still trying to get his Kalashnikov to fire. Jack turns his attention to the tarmac which is tearing toward him. He begins to stand as the roof below his feet gives way sending him falling to the level below. He hits the second floor hard, the ceiling falling in around him.

Where the ceiling used to be is a perfectly blue sky and nothing else. Debris continues to drop. Jack can just make out a child covered in rubble, still embracing the woman in black garb—their bodies crushed by the remains of the floor above.

The sound of heavy boots stomp nearby in the smoke.

Jack looks again to the hole above, searching for a glimpse of the boy and strange orb. His eyelids grow heavy. The room about him spins and fades, darkening beyond his control. He can hear a voice, echoing as if far away. Someone grabs his arm. He can barely feel the touch of fingers on his neck as the room goes black.

"This guy's still alive," the voice says.

THE BURNING PATH

The People of the Two Suns were as gods to us. Like us in base, but unlike in all that matters. When I was a girl I would go to the places that they created and marvel in the glory of their works. Their structures touched the clouds, made of stuff from faraway and deep beneath the ground. And everything that came from them we considered holy. I would wake and behold new temples of a greatness that bested the efforts of all my kind as one. And all that they made, they made for us.

"They leave these gifts," my mother had said when I was young, "for us to know our worth."

"But why, mother?" I badgered. "They are great and we are small."

She picked me up and I put my arms around her slender neck. Her long, dark hair was silk against my cheek. We turned to revel in the majesty of the great city upon the hills with its monoliths of tribute, gifted by the ones considered above all others. Their devices of flight speckled the distant sky as dark as ravens, should they fly a path as straight as shadow.

"The answer is in the gift," she said.

She suffered long in a body that seemed always at odds with her surroundings, dying quietly on a summer day of my fourteenth year. For all the powers the Great Ones had, they seemed not to bother with our mortality.

"Even death is a gift," my father had taught me. "From it we learn to wonder."

In my fifteenth year the Great Ones vanished. They left behind none of their implements of building. If ever they had dead, they left no hint. This day became known as the Day of Parting.

To the east, in the endless plains of grass, there stood now an edifice of gold, sized no greater than a coffer; four capped walls of four-barrels width and eight-barrels height. A band of embossed glyphs wrapped the upper periphery depicting a male and female holding hands. The design spanned all four sides, repeating itself in a seamless band— boy, girl, boy, girl, boy, girl ... The pious and the puzzled gathered around it, calling it the Parting Gift. On the west face was an opening of six-barrels height that led into a darkness from which no light could escape. My father held my hand amidst the crowd keeping us at a distance, as was his cautious way.

The first to enter was a soldier. He was a hero known to all, young and bold. My cousin giggled with her youthful lust as he passed, resplendent in his polished armor. Soon another followed in to retrieve the first. Then two more were sent, trembling, never to be seen again. For nine days, the people ushered all manner of creature into the dark entry of this curious remembrance—fowl and beast, feathered and scaled—yet none returned.

"Around this gift we shall erect a great temple," the High Prefect declared. "And we shall call it the Gate of the Two Suns. And through it we shall give fine and terrible tribute with each cycle of the seasons."

And so it was that the offerings began.

My father died in my seventeenth year leaving his business of trade to my husband, to whom I was promised the previous spring. My heart longed for the warmth of my mother's embrace and the security of my father's hands, but my new husband was a good man and one day he would give his life in exchange for my own. Textiles and animals were got from little known and far-off lands, made for sale by merchants under employment of my husband. These goods were sent by land and sea to the populations in the north where the appetite for such extravagances was great.

This was the second year of offerings to the new temple and a lottery was to be drawn of all the young between four and eleven years. The inaugural ceremony was given a boy of ten years, with golden locks and fair skin. His hair was adorned with flowers from the temple gardens, grown with care for such occasions. The monks of the Gate of the Two Suns stood the boy before a hushed crowd while the Lord of the Gate spoke words at great length, which I failed to hear from my position. I imagine he spoke of the Great Ones who created our highest temples, then abandoned us in the dead of night, but the zeal he displayed seemed fit more for the coming of war. After he spoke, the monks anointed the boy with oils applied to his brow. A garland was placed around his neck and a bouquet of violet placed within his arms. And all the while the boy stood silent, without a hint of fear. I wondered then, as I do now, what the boy was told. Did he believe that he was going to a land where children were kings and princely was the life of all things? Or was he told that he would play the hero in a story of cretins and beasts, and weapons and great feats? And would each child be told the same tale or would they be told something newly crafted to ease them into submission? Or maybe they would be told nothing at all. Maybe when they turned the golden-haired boy to face the dark entry of the Parting Gift, he was told simply to walk forward—and he did. Now, one could argue that a doorway leading to an infinite nowhere would best serve as a bin for civic waste, not as a graveyard for our children. Yet who could deny the Great Ones their tribute? So, in the boy walked with shoulders back and head held high, never to be seen again. It is rumored that the bereaved family was compensated in some way, but to what degree seems irrelevant. My own girl would be eligible for the lottery in two cycles of the seasons and no amount of gold could mend my ruptured soul should the gods be so inclined to take her.

By the time the second lottery was drawn I was in a prefecture twenty days north by bridled beast, accompanied by a fair train of servants and cargo. My daughter was left in the care of a nursemaid and my husband was waylaid by a sickness which bound him to our home. He bade me, "Take our goods northward to the Land of Moss and part with all at just price to those known well to this family." The routine was not unknown to me for I had accompanied my father to the northern lands on two occasions past. Our chief steward managed the caravan and I was to lend a sense of *familia* to any deals that be made, although I had little experience to offer in matters of such trade. "Not to worry," my husband assured me. "Jacob is a fine man and will no doubt secure any trade for us at good profit. You need only attend to represent our name."

"You would send me afar to suffer marauders," I joked, "when a signet would serve the purpose?"

He laughed and pulled me down to lie upon the bed with him as I feigned a desperate struggle.

"I pity the bandit who would come upon a harpy such as you!" he said, tickling me into submission until a fit of cough drew away his playful spirit.

***

The High Mountain of my home was behind the horizon but a gathering of distant cloud did hint at her position. When I passed this place as a child there had been a great stone archway that spanned the breadth of the road and rose many stories high, capped with pennants to name the many lands that mingle in these parts. The Great Ones had built this many lives ago as a marker to travelers announcing they were entering the lands of the pious counsels, those who above all else gave honor to the Ones from the Sky. The archway stood for a time before my father's father could remember, but now there stood only a pile of rubble to each side of the road.

"Who could do such a thing," I asked Jacob as we left the ruins to our backs. "Was there war?"

"Many things have changed since you were a child," he replied.

I could see a great wall of immeasurable size rise from beyond the hills, far before us.

"What is this?" I asked further. "I don't recall the city being fortified in such a way?"

"No ma'am. This is new to me, as well. Much has changed, indeed," Jacob said in matching surprise as we neared the great city of my cousins.

It had been fifteen days journey to reach the Land of Moss, and five more still to come upon the city of Kharal. Once there, I left the beasts under the care of a cousin's stable on the border of town, taking with me only the personal baggage to bed at a reputable inn near the market square where our business would soon commence. Our steward, Jacob, would lodge with familiars at a humble tenancy known as the Plaza and the twenty-so convoy hands would stay at a servants' hostel just west of the stables.

Kharal was then a large city of one-hundred and twenty-thousand souls, near thrice the population of my home to the south. Here the streets were wide and straight, and all led like wagon spokes to the civic center. Homes of repute were fed water from aqueducts which stretched some thirty days to the snowy mountains to the east. The refuse of the populous was drawn away at regular intervals, regardless of station, to stave the creatures known to harbor disease. As a result, the quality of air was exceptional for a metropolis, and the envy of all visiting envoys.

Jacob arrived at sunrise with the day's goods for trade, set upon three of our fifteen wagons. Linens got from the coastal towns of the Southern Sea were rolled tight at twenty-barrels breadth and several hundred of length. A count of fifty such rolls of various shades and hues could stack upon a single cart. All one-hundred and fifty were to be delivered to a notable merchant, and family friend, known formally as "Haegee." In my time, close friends of parents were addressed as kin, so an extended family could consist of countless "aunts" and "uncles," given a household's popularity. My name follows a deep lineage, even more so than my husband's, and so our bonds are wide.

Haegee greeted us without entourage as our train passed through the gates of his sizeable estate.

"Good graces! Meonas, is that you?" he asked, arms raised in greeting as our wagons came to a stop before him.

"It is, dear uncle. Do you not recognize the daughter of your dearest friend?"

"Nay! I do not!" he shouted playfully, extending a hand to help me from my seat. "I expected to see a funny little girl, with hair braided down to her knees. But you ... you are a woman! And a beauty, at that!"

I took Haegee by the hand and he aided me down to his side.

"And Jacob! My good, good friend!" my honorary uncle continued. "How nice it is to see your face. You, I know well. You look as you did when last we met, some five seasons ago. Old and stiff."

Jacob, a dour but loyal man, smiled for the first time since setting out.

"Aye, my lord," he replied. "I was born old and older yet I shall die."

Haegee turned, taking me by the shoulders.

"*My lord*, he calls me! I fought alongside his father in the bloodiest battles before time can recall, and he calls me *my lord*! Now that is a man that lives well within his station!"

Three servants approached and boarded the wagon without a word, knowing their task and their place. Jacob greeted them with a simple nod and let them to their business of assessing the cargo to determine which of the many houses of the estate to send each carriage.

"How is Prumeo, your father?" he asked of Jacob. "Has he breath left in him?"

"Aye, my lord. He will die when he is good and ready and not a moment before."

"Obstinate to the end, that man," Haegee laughs, directing the wagon train through the gates with a wave of his hand.

As the cargo moves past, Haegee takes my hand and gestures for me to walk with him. Servants close the iron gates behind. The lane leading to the estate is lined on either side with the most beautiful trees I had ever gazed upon and I inquire as to their type.

"They are blossoms of various breed, I think," my uncle replies, "imported, of course, from an island on the ass-end of the world. Your aunt can certainly shed a finer light than I. She is versed in all things born of earth, or so one would guess with all the dirt beneath her nails."

I admired the tiny, pink flowers billowing in the breeze, floating like downy matter to line the path before us. "They are heavenly," I say, almost below my breath.

"Well, you came at just the time. Like all beautiful things, their life is but a wink. Soon they will be all branch and twig. It's no wonder why Hermea planted them in so prominent a location, but their luster is fleeting. All of our occasions must be had between the fourth and fifth month or our guests will think I've left my home in shambles."

As we walked I felt comforted by the soft brush of blossom petals over my feet. I looked again to the great home at the end of the lane and remembered of the road to Kharal.

"What has become of the great archway to the city?" I asked. "And of the magnificent temples that stood on the hills? Have they fallen to ruin since I last came? It seems not so long ago."

Immediately I regretted the subject, seeing Uncle's mouth turn from smiles to grit. He looked at me then chose to focus on the trees before he spoke.

"You have been away from Kharal for too long, my niece," he began. "Much has changed in the minds of her people. Since the Great Ones abandoned us we have now the unaccustomed need to protect ourselves."

"Protect yourselves? From what?" I asked.

"From others, I suppose. From the elements," he answered, gesturing to the world around us. "But mostly from ourselves."

I held back a smile, sensing him to be aging and infirm in his sense, but knowing well that Haegee is a man who moves lightly until a hard wind blows. "What is there to be fearful of, dear uncle? Can we not govern ourselves?"

"We have dismantled the old complex of tribute and used the stone to build the great and terrible wall around our city. All of the monuments and all of the temples to the People of the Sky have been scavenged to dust from the collective mistrust of the unknown. The people of Kharal feel as orphans, alone and unsure. In place of temples to honor the Great Protectors we have erected a towering wall to a god called *Fear*."

"But how then is tribute given?" I asked. "Who of you calls to the Great Ones to return?"

Haegee lets out a laugh and catches fast my gaze. "Return?" he chides. "Why would they return?"

"But we are their beloved. Else why would they have propped us up above all others?"

He subdues another bout of agitated cheer, but wipes a tear from his eye in restraint. "We mean nothing to them. They have given us more than we could fathom, but took with them more than we could tell. Great canyons lie where earth once lay and hills are bare where only generations lost can recall the woods. They took what they came for, to return here nevermore."

"How can you know this?" I bade. "What we have been given could not have been wrought by the low. Ever grateful should our people be."

"My dear girl, they have given a pair of sandals to a one-legged man."

Just as I thought to inquire of my 'aunt', Hermea, she appeared in the portico of the great house before us. She lifted her gown above her feet with one hand and raised the other in greeting as she cared to descend the granite steps. Her beauty and grace would make one think her an empress.

"Meonas, my dearest niece!"

"Most loving aunt!"

At the base of the steps Hermea embraced me and kissed my lips. I took her hands in mine and playfully examined her fingers, then looked to my uncle. "Clean as polished gems," I played.

Uncle Haegee smiled at me in a disapproving way, but, upon catching the curious look of his wife, ushered us inside.

"You'll have time for jokes at feast," he said, slyly poking at my ribs.

***

Three great pillars on each side supported the upper floors of the great hall where the mid-day banquet was held. A "feast", indeed, of no less than twenty varieties of roasted fowl and cloven beast presented atop a masterfully crafted table, stretching from one end of the hall to the other. Much of the food appeared so ornate in presentation that I questioned whether it was to be eaten at all. The table itself was set with fifteen chairs to each side of mean length (with another on each end), but I counted just as many guests, if not far more, standing about in joyous conversation and manic ingestion as were formally seated. In all, there were in excess of eighty in the hall, with many more lingering about the grounds in various states of merry-making.

Aunt Hermea had mentioned earlier that the occasion for such splendid revelry was to celebrate my visitation, but considering that my relation to the countless guests (both familiar and familial) was non-existent, I supposed the truth of the matter was that Hermea simply enjoyed throwing a good party. Excuses be damned. I had little knowledge of who these people were, but I was happy to get to know them. However, the opportunity to make new acquaintances amongst the wealthy of Kharal would never quite present itself.

I had eaten my fill and drank more than planned when I spotted Jacob outside at the edge of the terrace landing, admiring the view of the vineyard countryside which stretched almost to the horizon. Although Jacob was bred a servant, his father's history with Uncle Haegee spanned greater than fifty years, and those years were born of the kind of perils that form bonds everlasting. To Haegee, Jacob was kin and welcome to join the festivities. But to Jacob, born from generations of servitude, it was old wisdom to keep his hands to his sides and his thoughts to himself. I rose from the table to join Jacob outside when Haegee repeatedly clanked a knife to his glass to gather our attention.

"Friends! Family!" my uncle began, taking a gulp from his glass to finish it off. "Thanks to all, from distant lands and unfamiliar shores ..."

Again, I peered out to Jacob who stood outside, looking away and to the hills. The attention of all was focused in toward Haegee giving his talk of welcome and gratitudes, but the focus of my family steward was fixed upward and to the distance. It was a warm and beautiful day, the light only then beginning to fade to a scheme of soft pinks, much like the blossoms of the lane. The clouds were high and few. I followed Jacob's gaze to the distance, catching the true object of his thoughts.

The object was without motion in the sky, and distant, before the hills that lined the horizon, but beyond the endless orchard rows and vines of fruit. It was smooth and shaped as almonds are, at a dozen barrels height and twice more for width. It took on the shade of the sky, but I knew its true color to be that of a mirror of polished silver. There could be no doubt as to its nature. This was unnatural art that could only be forged by the People of the Two Suns. I stood to exit the hall, but was met with heavy applause.

"Dear, Meonas! They cheer for you!" Haegee shouted to me from across the table and above the din of clapping (and now laughter). Apparently I missed my gracious introduction as the most honored of guests. I again looked out toward Jacob and, further still, to the orb of silver in the distant sky, neither noticed by any but Jacob and me.

"My niece is overcome with gratitude!" Haegee added, filling in the silence for my lack of reply.

My legs felt to be undone with sudden weakness. The great hall appeared to sway. I thought immediately of the berry wine of which I had two glasses—*or was it more*? But I am not so susceptible to port as one would think!

A scream was let from across the room, and then another. Then the crowd shifted in attention to the white pillars which began to crack at their length. The ground shifted violently, this way and the next, sending huddled groups to the floor and others running for an exit. More screams cut through the heavy sound of earth, in debilitating flux beneath our feet, with confused shouts as the plaster from the ceiling began to fall as if held too long by warm candle wax.

Many found sanctuary under the great dining table while others in flight were crushed by the collapse of walls or lighting fixtures that detached from the ceiling to impale their targets like iron lances.

I, too, took refuge under the great table as the whole of the estate seemed to be crumbling away into rubble.

***

I felt a rough hand grab firm my arm through the cloud of dirt and plaster dust, then coughed without relent as Jacob pulled me from beneath the table and to my feet. He ushered me out to the yard with great haste, lest the earth begin to quake once more. There I turned back to witness the horror of Haegee's stately manor, flattened as if stepped on by the foot of the God King himself.

The sky around had darkened in a cloud. Warm, gray flakes settled onto my shoulders from above. Jacob bade me to turn again to the hills in the distance, and so I did. The silver orb hung silent still, beyond the fields, but now aligned with this was a great and fearsome column of black smoke which rose up beyond measure and belief, parting the highest of clouds to form an oaken silhouette energized with the bolts of heaven enraged. I believed then that we stood witness to the end of all time.

Jacob looked at me and braced my arms in his hands to take my attention for himself.

"That is the High Mountain of your home, Madam!" he howled over the din of an angry countryside.

"No, it cannot be," was my feeble reply.

"The great mark of your country is no more. The gods have split the earth at the seams. We must look to your home without delay."

Thoughts of my daughter and husband heated my mind. I could not believe from this sight that any would survive such hell-wrought calamity as the forceful disruption of an entire mountain. Wiping the dirt from my eyes, I replied, "Yes, Jacob, we must see to our families. Yours and mine." I then turned back toward the destruction that was once the great and noble estate of a dear family friend. "But first we will tend to those near."

The silver orb had vanished from the sky, and I would never see another.

***

Haegee was dead. Like many others in the city of Kharal, he was crushed by the artificial surroundings they created to protect themselves. More still had been burned alive in the maelstrom of fire and violence that followed. All that stood were the few structures left by the People of the Two Suns, now protruding triumphantly from the wreckage of the once great city as a reminder of our inferiority. The magnificent defensive wall erected by the denizens of Kharal had fallen in the course of a breath.

Jacob and I traveled south on bridled beast. With nothing left of our merchandise to barter (and hardly a soul alive to barter with), my resourceful family steward managed, miraculously, to procure our transport and enough rations to last five days. I did not ask Jacob how he came about our necessities and I did not question the road ahead. And we did not discuss the dismal odds of ever reaching my home alive.

Our food was no more after only four days slow travel, not from gluttony but from spoil. The rank cloud of darkness that enveloped the land had seeped into our goods and turned them to poison. Our faces were covered by scarves of tattered linen and the linen covered in a gray soot that had repeatedly dampened, then hardened, from the morning mists. The air thickened with ash each day, aggravating the senses, leaving navigation a matter of blind memory. None of the constructed landmarks lay bare to mark the way. Our only fortune was the river that ran from the north along our route. With cloth to strain the debris, we had ample enough water to keep us. There was little sense to clean our clothes with the ashen sky at a persistent downfall (and the mud provided a layer of gate against the chill). I left my life to the wisdom of Jacob, who I obeyed without question in these matters of survival.

We had not set eyes on the sun since the High Mountain erupted. An accurate account of days was nearly impossible with the perpetual night that engulfed and confounded us. We sustained ourselves by siphoning the blood of our weakest beast through a cut made along the neck, then bandaged and re-opened when thirst and want had overcome us. With the mercy of the gods, the animal lived to provide us comestible enough for several days before it could walk no more. Jacob cooked and dried the beast in fillets a size to travel and we continued on after two or more days. My companion and guide seemed to me too generous in his aid and took little for himself in all things of need. And after more days than I care to know, and the fall and rationing of our second bridled beast, we reached the edge of my lands.

The indestructible invention of the People of the Two Suns were the only structures which still stood. All else, the low craft of mortals, had disappeared beneath a sea of ashen spew, deeper than a temple's spire.

We could proceed no farther. Beneath the deep soot lay a sort of liquid earth which burned red, then cooled to a smooth rock that emitted a poisonous smoke. I could only guess at the hill that held my home by relating the position of the remaining monuments of the Sky Folk. And on that hill, nothing lay but ruin.

"There is nothing left for me here, dear friend," I said to Jacob as he took my hand to comfort me. "We should leave at once to your father's land and pray he fares better."

"Aye, Madam," he replied, tenderly wiping the ash from my hand. He must have expected my tears to follow, but none did. I have had many days to contemplate the fate of my husband and daughter on this long journey home, and so the truth brought no surprise. My land was razed with such ferocity and haste that none within its borders could escape. Yet ...

At that moment we could hear the faint, but continual ring of a bell, such that is worn by cattle. But it was not beast that sounded the call, but a man (from what I could tell at my vantage) standing on a distant plateau where the Gate of the Two Suns once lay. His arm was raised high, clanging for our attention. I turned again to Jacob whose brows furrowed and lips formed something of a smile. What an unexpected thing, he must have thought.

We maneuvered two or three fields east on the periphery of the city to reach the buried trail to the top of the plateau. At this higher point the soot came only above my feet and was moved upon with little effort, and the soft warmth of the ash felt oddly comforting, for the morning air was cold. I could see the dark gray mounds created by the settlement of mountain spew atop the ruins of the temple, once called the Gate of the Two Suns. And at the center of the ruins was the little man, still ringing his bell in steady time to guide our way through the smoldering decay.

The bellman's cloak was black, but, curiously, not from ash. His hands were impossibly free of grime; his skin, alabaster and feminine. With the removal of his hood, I recognized him at once to be the golden-haired boy who was made sacrifice, here at the Gate of the Two Suns over a year ago. He wore, still, the garland placed around his neck by the Keepers of the Gate, just before they ushered him inside the golden entryway, never to be seen again.

Well, "never" until now.

It was then that I noticed the faint shine of metal hidden below the ash and debris that covered the golden doorway— or Parting Gift. Like all else composed by the People of the Two Suns, it had withstood heavenly catastrophe.

"How did you come to be here, boy?" Jacob inquired, turning his attention to the unholy darkness of the Gift.

Ash continued to settle lightly on the boy's golden hair, but he paid no mind. He smiled and looked into my eyes.

"This one is Meonas," he stated plainly. "I have come for her."

Jacob turned and met my surprise.

"Me?" I replied, quite unsure of the boy's intentions.

"Who has sent you?" Jacob added.

"Have you come from beyond the gate?" I asked, examining again his unsoiled vestments. "The falling earth has not yet found you."

The golden-haired boy extended his smile, and his thoughts seemed older than his years. "Your daughter waits for you, Meonas."

Daughter? My heart raced. I nearly lost my legs, but Jacob took my arm to keep me still.

To my protector, the prospect of commuting through a dark, uncharted void to reunite with loved ones must have seemed suspect, and Jacob let his mind be known.

"Madam, think on it a while," he urged, looking again to the boy. "Many have entered that infernal hole, chosen and beast, yet none have since returned."

The boy, with his smile subdued, looked about at the ruins of the once great land and saw nothing but ash and smoke blowing from a mountain alight with fire.

"Would you?" he asked, with a sensible quality of voice that set my thoughts at ease. "This world is fouled."

"But, Madam ..." Jacob began, searching for his words or waiting for mine.

"Know this, Meonas," the boy addressed me, emanating a tangible aura as if unnaturally laden with wisdom. "The High Mountain has not yet completed its death knell. In short order it will again put forth a mighty throw that will bury this realm in stone and coal, and shroud the door for a time much beyond telling."

Jacob squeezed my hand to speak his mind without wasting words.

"The time to reunite with your daughter is now," the boy urged with sincerity. "Or never again."

I looked to Jacob. The apprehension in his gaze gave way to understanding. How could he ask me to keep from my daughter? This golden-haired boy was proof enough that the dark gateway, given by the People of the Two Suns, was more than just a pit for sacrifice to appease and plead to a race of beings beyond our comprehension. I had witnessed this very boy ushered into the Gift more than a year past, yet here he stands before me, lucid and unharmed. This doorway was a means to save my people, but little did we know. And now, with a way in hand, what mother would not risk life to save her child? To nurture family? To be with the ones they love? Those who need them most.

I looked to the boy and he returned my smile as if knowing my mind. I looked to the sky above, roiling in thunder and devilish hue. I looked to the High Mountain, blowing at the air with fire and cinder. The ancient lands of my kin, covered in ash and liquid rock. And I looked finally to my dear friend and companion who has served my family at the expense of his own.

My hand held Jacob's and I walked onward, toward the Parting Gift and nearer to my daughter. The cloaked boy stepped aside to open my way, but Jacob gently released his hand from mine, letting our fingers slide apart. He stopped as I turned back to ask the matter, and he just looked into my eyes with that stone gaze that never gave his mind.

"This one cannot enter," the golden-haired boy said, looking to me but speaking of my companion. "He is not of our kind."

Jacob did not speak to defend himself, which was just his quiet way, as the consummate attendant.

"Rubbish!" I exclaimed, louder than warranted. "Jacob is not merely a servant, he is a dear friend and my great protector on this terrible quest. He stands before me in all things. Station be damned!" I smiled just slightly, a bit ashamed of my enthusiasm for I lacked the flare for the dramatic. But heavens be bled if it were not true, and more. I turned to Jacob, half expecting him to blush from such affections, although I knew better than to want for displays of emotion from such a stern man.

"The boy is correct, My Lady," Jacob began, before I could let my feelings take control.

"Rubbish!" slipped again from my lips. "None of this 'My Lady' nonsense today. I will not leave you to suffer a lung full of ash and cinder. We shall leave this place together."

Impervious to my rants, the boy looked to Jacob with brows high, meeting his gaze with a subtle familiarity. "She does not know?"

I too, turned to my friend, never being one for secrets. "Know what?"

Before Jacob could speak, the boy gave answer. "By design, the gate can only be crossed by living flesh. Your companion," he paused, looking to Jacob as if asking permission to continue, "is *Diord-na*."

All went silent to me, as if the gods themselves had held my ears between their palms and squeezed. My mind sped to other times when the People of the Two Suns populated the land with their fantastic devices of motion and flight. They erected towers that could eat the sun's grace and shine throughout the night, and tiles as hard as stone that were invisible to the eye. I had been told stories of the Diord-na as a girl, but it seemed too surreal to believe, even for a child. They were not as we are, spawn of this earth from mother and father, but wrought by the masterly hands of the Great Ones themselves. In visage they are more like than unlike, but in mind they are the effect of their masters. What purpose they serve is not to my understanding. These are fables. I cannot believe it.

"Rubbish," I said, wondering when I last spoke that word so often.

"It is true, My Lady," Jacob replied softly, pulling up the sleeves of his cloak. Between the thumb and finger of his left hand he pinched the middle finger of the other. A quick twist and his finger was knuckle-side down. He pushed it back, with a truly unnerving, fleshy ratcheting sound, until it lay fully against the back of his hand.

What is this gruesome sight?! Jacob's finger was nearly broke free, without so much as a grimace on his face.

"Rubb—"

Jacob then detached his right hand with a quick turn at the wrist and, as a courtesy, held it out for me to see. *Heavens be felled!* I witnessed no blood dripping to the ground. His detached hand lay in the palm of the other, yet the fingers wiggled about with unnerving intention, not in displays of painful spasm, but neatly tapping each finger to the tip of the thumb with the rhythm of counting. One, two, three, four, three, two, one, two, three, four ... until I could look no more and raised my gaze to Jacob's.

"Diord-*na*," he said to me, raising his handless arm a bit to give me a good (if not wholly unsolicited) look inside the disjoined ending.

I did not know what I witnessed, and still do not. Jacob did not bleed. It was not bone. It was not flesh. But it moved ever-so slightly as if wanting for its departed hand.

"Diord-na, indeed," I replied, before losing my legs and falling into temporary darkness.

I will posit here, and leave it be, that I would not have fainted had I been well nourished. And, moreover, the perpetual fall of ash had affected my sense. Can any challenge this? Aye, but with little heart. It can be argued that the rank air and graying meats did more to unbalance me than the sight of Jacob's dancing severed hand. Know, I once stood witness to three soldiers beheaded on a summer day with a blunt axe, and as gruesome as it was, it failed to reverse my digestion. As for this spell upon me now, it lasted only moments before my sense was righted and questions rose to center.

"But you have a father and a mother?" I began my inquiry as Jacob lifted me to my feet. "How can you be a device of the People of the Two Suns? I have known you since I was a girl. I have seen you age!"

"You are still a girl," Jacob replied, with no harm in his voice. "Have you really seen me age? You are not yet twenty years. Much less. I have been known to you and your husband's family not yet nine years. Even a man of flesh would have changed little in this time."

"But you have an earthly father, Prumeo, who is like kin to Haegee, my bon-uncle. They have known great fear together and great love, through many ages. Do not disclose that I know not what I know." I did not want to hear what I guessed would be a very vexing reply.

"Prumeo and Haegee shared a true bond of many years, and to that I do not contradict. But Prumeo is not my father, for my kind are not born of earth and water. I am, many years times many, greater in age then both Haegee and Prumeo combined. I was wrought when those you call the People of the Two Suns first made their existence known to this world. A time out of mind to you and yours. As I said to Haegee, 'I was born old and older yet I shall die,'" Jacob reminded.

The golden-haired boy stood patiently at the entrance to the Parting Gift, sensing well that I would never follow him into the gate with a mystery so great before me. I must know the truth of this, at the err of myself and kin. The mountain ash continued to fall, as it would so for many months, yet the boy did not don his hood. The earth-spew settled quietly upon his golden locks.

I was relieved to see that Jacob had placed his hand back where it belonged, attached to his arm, and beneath his sleeve.

"But why in heaven's balls have you spent these past years looking to my stables and washing my family's soiled beddings? Surely there are greater tasks at hand for the manufactured progeny of the Great People." I nearly yelled, so perplexed I was by this development.

"I am your steward, My Lady. I do not directly care for the family stables or soiled beddings, but I see your meaning."

"Oh, rubbish! Get on with it."

Jacob shook the ash from his shoulders. "The family of Prumeo had served the Great Ones well through the line of many descendants. In return, I was given to serve the father of Prumeo's father. Upon his passing, I served the father of Prumeo, then Prumeo. And in his late age, Prumeo did instruct me to serve the family of his dear friend, Haegee, for Prumeo has no true heirs. Prumeo thinks more for his friends than for himself. He wished to see me serve your family well before passing. And he has, I believe."

"So, my uncle Haegee knew of your deep origins?"

"No, My Lady. Haegee did only know me as the son of Prumeo, his friend in war and in peace. But Haegee, being one of magnificent wealth, had little need for another steward. Although, had he known my making he may have thought differently. So I was bade to call upon your husband's family to do them aid so, through me, Haegee could keep loving watch over his distant cousin, your father by marriage."

"I confess that without you as steward my husband could not have had the means or the cunning to advance his trade. He is a kind man, with many fine qualities, but he has no head for business. He has spoken of your contributions many times with great affection." I noticed again the chill of the air and saw that the light of the sky had dimmed with the hour. For all his good manner, I sensed that the golden-haired boy must be growing weary of my delay.

I continued my interrogation. "But how, by the gods, have you not been found out? If you do not age as we do, I can hardly believe ..."

"I am believed to be the son of a servant, who is born to a long line of servants," Jacob answered. "None of high station care to know my family line. In ten generations, no noble or high caste has ever asked of my history, save for you now."

I pondered this a moment. I knew Jacob's "father," Prumeo, only by name, but to my dire recollection, I never spoke to Jacob much beyond platitudes.

"In due time, if not for the events that thrust this world into darkness, I would have disclosed my true self to your family," he continued, "and together it would be no great matter to pass me as someone new every twenty years or so. The family of Prumeo is only one of many that I have served over the centuries. *A man of low station goes unseen in high places.*"

Damn the gods, for I knew this to be true. I could not recall, if ever I had asked, the names of my servant's children.

Then the earth shook. My legs felt weak and I held out my arm hoping to catch hold of a thing to brace. And, as he had many times in my youth and of late through this terrible time, Jacob came forward and held me steady.

But although the ground did quake with a temper to match the fall of Haegee's home, here there were no buildings left to topple. And so I stood, with not so much fear as before, until the hard movement below my feet subsided. And as if to beckon my tardy heart forward, the quake had shaken loose the heavy ash that covered the Parting Gift, revealing a glimmering monolith of ageless gold that sparkled red against the fiery sky.

Jolted from his patience the golden-haired boy resumed his solicitations. "Madam, we must not linger. I cannot hold the heavens back."

Even as the earth trembled I found it difficult to think of little more than the personage of loyalty who had guided me back to my daughter. "What are you to do, Jacob, my dearest friend?"

"I will go to where Prumeo last stood, and if he still breathes I will usher him to safer ground, if any there be. If he has fallen, I will bring him to the land of his fathers and lay him beneath the earth, as is your custom."

"I will come with you," I said stepping nearer to my friend, placing my hands in his. "Together we will claim dear Prumeo."

Jacob squeezed my fingers then let them slide free for the second time. "You would not survive the journey, My Lady. I am made of tougher stuff than you and need little in the way of sustenance. But you are flesh. The dark sky falls hard about us. There is no game or plant left to feed upon. Out here, in this world, you will not live beyond this day."

My soul felt to spill from my body, but I knew Jacob was right. What choice do I have?

"Go into the gate," he said. "Follow this boy. But be wary of what you find. Find your daughter and keep her close. Question those around you. Deny offers that seem more than deserved for all that glitters is not gold."

I kept my eyes hard upon Jacob's and almost swear that he met my smile with his own. He guessed, I suppose, that I would not leave him without that most cherished of gifts to remember him by. I turned finally to the golden-haired boy (whose hair was now gray with heavy soot) and removed the linen scarf from around my head. I fought hard against turning back for one last look at the friend who gave himself freely to generations of my kin. Instead I held my hand out to the patient boy and offered him a thankful smile and my humbled life. Saying simply, "Lead the way."

MICHAEL

Michael stares out the window of the Greyhound bus, watching the Oregon landscape scroll by. He is tired of just sitting all the way from San Francisco, but decides that pulling the shade down to get some sleep would be inconsiderate to the woman seated next to him. She is deep into a novel and he shouldn't deprive her of the afternoon sunlight. Natural light, he thinks, is a gift. He smiles, catching himself being sentimental.

The I-5 corridor between Eugene and Salem is an endless swath of pastoral fields and distant hills. From here it's a straight shot north, dotted with the occasional alpaca paddock and rest-stop dog park. Outside, the farmland stretches back for miles to some unreachable part of the world that no roads could possibly lead to. Michael wonders if he could ever settle in a place like this. Now forty, he is old enough to know who he is and old enough to appreciate the little time he has left. A place like this, far from the urban bustle, could be good for the soul.

This part of the country isn't unfamiliar to him. He had traveled this road many times to visit his sister in Portland, back when he had a car, back before things started to go wrong. His emotional state isn't what it used to be—if ever it was stable—and he is beginning to realize that friends alone can never be enough. He had let many go when their needs weighed too heavy on him, and now little can be expected in return. He needs to be close to his family again. He hasn't seen his mother in years and it's time to change all that. First to Portland and his sister, then to Seattle where his mother will welcome him and cap-off this meaningless decade of wandering.

The Greyhound pulls in for a scheduled stop at a gas station, not far off the main highway, in a place that could hardly pass as a truck stop. There is the road, and then there is farmland. It's a ten-minute opportunity for new passengers to board, old passengers to disembark, or the restless to just stretch their legs. Michael chooses a cigarette. It's only been forty minutes since the last stop in Eugene, but the minutes compound quickly when your energy is siphoned by the desperation of those around you. He wonders how much life he's stolen from the people who've known him too well. He lights up a smoke around the side of the building. *It must be ages.*

He takes a drag. The smoke fills his lungs and for a fleeting moment his cares step aside. A mouse shuffles near from around the corner, sniffing frantically at the concrete walkway. It noses about in circles searching for anything that might make a meal, or at least a nibble, but there is always nothing—just loose gravel and soiled cigarette butts. *Why have you come here? Where is your home?*

Michael has always felt emotionally tied to the destitute, relating more to creatures of the wild than to the people around him. He watches as the rodent turns back and loses itself in a field behind the dumpsters. Cigarette smoke rises, unnoticed, up to the skies.

The *beep-beep-beep* of his digital watch snaps him out of his trance.

***

The restroom is less than ideal. The usual filth lay strewn, languishing in puddles of sewage that soil the floor. Michael has a theory that the over-all sanitation of an establishment can be determined by the cleanliness of its lavatory. The restroom is always the last place a business cares for, so if the restroom is clean then so must the kitchen be. The converse is almost never the case. He opens his backpack producing a small leather pouch. Patrons can be heard converging outside, clamoring to use the toilet before the bus departs. Michael unzips the pouch and readies a syringe.

***

The bus driver checks his watch and takes another drag of his cigarette. He enjoys the unusually dry summer that Oregon has presented this year, but knows it can't last much longer. Too often has he driven this route through heavy rain and sunless days. The occasional deep snow was the worst. It meant that he would have to get out and affix the chains. Riders would get antsy. Babies would cry. And when he was ready to go, some guy would exit the bus, scampering down the road to find a place to pee. It's nearly time to go, but the passengers will have to wait until his smoke is fully cashed-out.

***

Michael brings a few ready-made sandwiches and a bottle of sugar-free soda to the counter. He grabs a Snickers bar from the impulse display and pays the cashier. Outside, the bus is loaded and ready to go. The driver guides a few stragglers up the steps and takes his seat behind the wheel.

Michael places the items in his backpack, standing at a distance from the bus's open door.

The passengers peer at Michael anxiously through the windows. He gazes at the blue sky that fills the whole of the earthly periphery and wonders at the beauty of this world. Crops of grain brush quietly in the summer breeze. Somewhere far in the distance a train blows its whistle and continues slowly on to other places. But something is missing. Something is not right. Michael feels a familiar tug on his soul that tells him to alter his course and explore his surroundings. *How can I let this elegance escape me*? He was never one for following a plan. Plans keep you sheltered. Schedules stunt your imagination. He decides that his family would have to wait a little longer.

The bus driver places his hand on the door lever and motions to Michael. "It's time to go, my friend."

Michael throws the backpack squarely over his shoulders and smiles. "It's a beautiful day. I think I'll walk."

The driver returns a smile and seems to understand in a way that borders on envy. There are few people in this world that live their lives as if they are truly free, the rest are just observers. He closes the door and eases the bus forward, toward the open road, and away.

Follow the mouse. That's Michael's new plan. Around the corner and through a field of tall grass. Just follow the mouse. Beyond a lonely dirt road and down a soft embankment. Past cows grazing in the sun and industrial sprinklers watering their fields. Follow the mouse to somewhere other than where he is now and someplace special that he's never been. He could feel his heart lighten with every step. People are waiting for him, but it doesn't matter. They know him well enough. They know that he is guided by impulse. That the journey above all else, is his only reward. The beauty of the world is meant to be experienced. People, with their expectations and their daily planners, can wait.

***

The train tracks roll ahead of him for miles without a bend in sight, but the landscape rises and falls about in waves. He walks between the rails taking his time, admiring the trees and quiet sounds that were once drowned by the mechanical buzz that choke the now distant highway. Here his mind is free to languish in the natural forms that lost their place when stones became structures and letters supplanted memories. He walks north toward some ultimate land, kicking playfully at some cans along the railroad.

***

Michael walks for miles before thinking that a drink would do him well. He swings his pack around onto one shoulder and continues ahead, digging around inside for that soda he had stowed away. Deep down, between a mess of T-shirts and socks, the bottle lay wrapped within a plastic shopping bag. He looks up, soda in hand, and stops.

From nowhere, it seems, a man appears before him.

The man is in his twenties, disheveled and unwashed. The whites of his eyes are red from tears. He returns Michael's gaze with unease. The man looks in shock, as if he had just witnessed a horrible accident.

Michael forces a smile and extends his hand, offering his soda in a gesture of goodwill.

The man takes a step closer, placing a hand on Michael's shoulder. He plunges a knife deep into Michael's abdomen, closing his eyes tightly, afraid to see what he's just done.

The bottle falls from Michael's hand.

The man pulls Michael close, locking him in a tight embrace, ear-to-ear. Tears well in the man's eyes, seeping through his clenched lids.

Michael grabs at the man's shoulders to brace himself. His backpack drops to the ground.

The man opens his eyes and gazes, teary-eyed, at the immeasurable landscape. Hills embrace the open skies. Tall pines pin the two together. It's a gift from gods for mortal joy, but the beauty seems to torture him. He pushes the knife further in.

Michael struggles for air, eyes wide, clutching feebly at the man. The landscape pitches and blurs before him. His grip gives way and he slides slowly down.

The man frees the knife with a swift tug and takes a step back. He wipes his tears on his sleeve. Blood streaks his brow.

Michael falls to his knees and then to his side, his head resting on the ground. The side of his face presses against the whetted gravel.

"I'm sorry," the man repents, then hurries away.

Michael lies motionless on his side, each breath heavier than the last. Heavy lids half cover his watery eyes. His breath disturbs the ground beneath his lips. Tears seep down off the bridge of his nose, falling just inches to the dirt. He blinks to clear his sight, moving his labored gaze up and to the distance before him. He blinks again with a look of disbelief. Struggling, he tilts his head from off the ground, fighting for a better view. His breathing slows and calms.

A shape can be seen—dulled but reflective—just yards away, hovering above the train tracks, waiting as if interested in Michael's condition; noiseless, motionless and completely out of place.

Jack and Dr. Abbott

Market Street glistens from the early morning memory of light June rain. The parting clouds open to blue sky, hopelessly prodded by the towering buildings of downtown San Francisco. Jack sits quietly in the back of the taxi, looking out the window as the city bustles with activity. Denizens congregate on the cobblestone thoroughfare of the United Nations Plaza. Students enter and exit the modern structure of the city library. Vagrants drink their contraband from re-used paper bags. Shopping carts and bicycles line the nearby shoulder of the esplanade. Tourists at Powell Street clutch sacks of memorabilia, waiting in line for cable cars to take them away from the punk-rock junkies panhandling for change outside the Gap. Street vendors hock their wares. Montgomery Street suits sip lattes, clutching mobile phones and presumably making deals with clients on the eastern coast. Who else could they be calling to so early in the morning? Commuters pour out from the underground B.A.R.T. stations, coming off trains that transport the enumerable souls from the Bay Area suburbs to the frantic urban grind.

The taxi turns left at Ferry Plaza. Jack seems content, unaffected, his hand resting on the duffel bag beside him. He smiles, taking in the morning as the taxi approaches the Marina Harbor.

Two men are visible on the deck of a 50ft fishing boat moored at the end of the nearest pier. They busy themselves loading equipment and rations, preparing the boat for launch. On the rear of the boat is "The Janet's Doll", written in a large cursive font of gold and black trim. They wave a greeting to Jack as he exits the taxi and pays his fare. Sea lions bask on an adjacent pier as if bound to the planks by the warmth of the sun.

One of the men meets Jack with a handshake as he steps off the ramp and onto the boat.

***

From the aft deck of *The Janet's Doll* the San Francisco skyline is an impressive display of glimmering glass and steel, shrinking slowly behind as the boat makes its way across the wide-open stretches of the bay.

The noon sky reflects in Jack's sunglasses as a distorted panorama of white clouds and coastline. He snaps off photos of the distant city, seated comfortably as the sea air brushes coolly against his skin. The Golden Gate Bridge dwarfs the fishing vessel as it passes under; a shiny white speck beneath the massive cathedral of blood-orange steel, bobbing out like a toy toward the open ocean. To the distant left is the Presidio which anchors the massive Golden Gate at Fort Point, a brick fortification erected to deter hostile incursion at the height of the California Gold Rush. Jack turns with a smile, the imposing towers behind, the salted wind blowing through his short brown hair.

***

Dr. Jeffery Abbott hands Jack a can of beer then seats himself on an adjoining deck chair. Seagulls caw, some bobbing in the water and others circling in the air, anticipating a netted catch or toss of remnant bait that this voyage isn't likely to deliver. Abbott cracks open a beer, sipping at it quickly as a heavy froth expands dripping from can, to hand, to cargo shorts.

"Shit," he laughs, holding out his beer to redirect the mess.

Jack turns his attention from the orange glow of the sunset as Abbott stands, wiping the beer from his legs.

"If it's not the damn seagulls, it's something else," Abbott complains, taking another sip, glaring at the birds circling wildly in the sky above the boat. "They're just flying rats."

Jack lifts his sunglasses onto his head, squinting to adjust his eyes to the light. "Aren't you supposed to love animals or something?" he asks.

Abbott raises a brow. "Not when they shit all over me."

Jack returns his gaze to the western horizon, sliding his sunglasses back onto his nose.

"Look at them," Abbott continues, pointing to the seagulls bobbing on the water. He has a glint of sunset in his dark brown eyes and a sly grin on his face. "These bastards will follow a fishing boat a hundred miles from shore just to get some scraps of bait. A hundred miles!" He takes another sip and wipes the moisture from his lips. "I had a girlfriend that had a cockatiel," he recalls. "She would let the little beast roam around the apartment when I wasn't home. She let it shit all over my pillow. Thought it was cute."

He motions like he's going to throw his beer into the water like a grenade, then takes another sip. "Fuck birds."

"Sounds like you chose the wrong profession, my friend," Jack says, closing his eyes and letting his head fall back in relaxation. Wisps of his hair flow in the breeze.

"Whales," Abbott responds, placing a hand on Jack's shoulder to steady himself. "Whales are the reason for my being, Jack. The sentinels of the sea. They're the key to you and me." He checks his watch.

"You don't say."

"I do. And, by the way, George and I thank you for taking the time from rollicking through global genocide to take a few pictures for us." He finishes off the last drop of beer then shakes the can just to be sure. "I appreciate it and the university appreciates it."

"Yeah? Jeffery, I'm touched."

"Well, maybe not the university, those cheap bastards, but I sure do." Abbott tosses his empty beer can into a bin and retakes his seat. "This boat stinks like rotten fish! This chair stinks like rotten fish. No wonder these flying rats followed us out here." He peers at the seagulls with disdain.

"It's a fishing boat," Jack reminds him.

"Not today, my friend. Today it's a vessel of pure science. You'd think they could hose it off every once in a while." Abbott reaches into a cooler and grabs another beer. "I have a very sensitive pallet."

Jack turns his head limply, still nestled on the back of his deck chair, relaxed enough to slide off. His hands rest on is mid, holding his untouched beer. "You really did pick the wrong profession."

Abbott takes a sip. "Not everyone can be a tough guy like you."

Jack smiles, turning his gaze back to the sunset which is half sunk into the ocean horizon. The orange sky has darkened, turning a gradient of red to black.

"Speaking of which," Abbott prompts, "how are you?"

"Great," Jack replies. "Got the setting sun and the salt sea air. I can't complain."

"Come on, Jack. You know what I mean."

Jack opens his eyes, noticing the seagulls have parted.

"How's your shoulder? How's your leg?" Abbott sits up and leans toward Jack, examining a scar that runs from above his left ear and down to the base of his skull. "How's that tiny brain of yours?"

"Fine." Jack grins to Abbott for reassurance. "Seriously. I think I'm actually smarter now."

"Of course you are," Abbott says, leaning back on his chair and taking a sip of beer. "You're a tough-guy."

Jack chuckles, noticing the glimmer of a star break through the evening veil. "That's right."

"An entire building lands on you and it's just another day at the office. You lead a charmed life, my friend." Abbott takes a sip. "You're the only guy I know that can get mauled by a tiger and walk out of the hospital with a bigger dick."

A man exits the boat's steering cabin and approaches along the starboard rail carrying a digital tablet which illuminates his upper half.

"They're coming our way," he announces, making adjustments to his display with a touch of a finger.

"Me and George, we're just regular guys," Abbott continues.

George looks at him with quiet exasperation.

"Jeffery," Jack responds. "You are anything but a regular guy."

Abbott stands, tossing his beer can into the bin and putting a stiff grip on Jack's shoulder.

"Come on, Jack," he says. "Let's go do some fucking science."

***

The Janet's Doll floats quietly twenty miles out to sea. The glow of the urban sprawl to the east can be seen like an artificial Arora blanketing the coast. Stars speckle the night sky. The faint cosmic strip of the Milky Way wraps itself around the planet. The moon, nearly full, reflects in the calm Pacific waters.

Orange lifejackets hang from hooks on the wood-paneled walls of the boat's main cabin. The ocean is dark, hardly visible through the windows that wrap the room on three sides. George checks his electronic tablet, scrolling through a digital representation of their location at sea. He touches the screen, sliding his fingers to expand and contract the map until the central icon of their point is adjacent to a cluster of red dots blinking near the top-right of the screen. Dr. Abbott places a set of large headphones over his ears, plugging its cord into a receptor on a portable recording device that rests on the cabin table. Several dials and needle indicators adorn the face. He plugs another corded device of black, flattened cylindrical plastic into the recording box then flips a switch to power it on.

"Testing, testing," he says, speaking into the cylindrical hydrophone. The needles on the box react to his voice with gentle spikes. He presses a button and a red recording light blinks. "George Lee is a sexy, sexy man."

Georges looks up from his tablet display, giving Abbott another in a long series of disapproving looks. He pulls open a Velcro-fastened compartment at the mid of his all-weather jacket, which then unfolds to form something of an apparel platform affixed to his body, held up by straps attached to his jacket breast. He places his tablet on the fabric platform, fastening it down with Velcro straps then twists his body left to right a few times to be sure the device is secure. Jack watches him with a smile. George looks like a high-tech peanut vendor without the bags of peanuts.

"I take that back," Abbott records into the hydrophone, gawking at the contraption on George's belly. "George Lee is destined to die a virgin."

Jack clicks the button of a handheld photometer then puts its strap over his head and around his neck. He powers on his camera to check for battery life, strapping that too around his neck. The bulk of the heavy 400mm lens doesn't seem to bother him as the strap tugs against his skin.

"They're about five miles out, northeast," George announces, enlarging the digital field of view with a spread of his fingers on the tablet display. "Time to go."

Abbott stops adjusting his gear and responds with an excited grin, looking to George who continues to ignore him, and then to Jack. "Time to go, Mr. Pace."

***

Silhouettes of resting seagulls bob against the reflection of the moon. George stands next to the port rail, scanning the dark expanse of the Pacific Ocean. Nothing can be seen but the urban glow to the east and a starry sky that blends itself seamlessly with the western horizon. Abbott leans over the railing, lowering the hydrophone carefully into the water, feeding down its long, rolled cable hand-over-hand.

Jack stands at the bow readying a set of portable flood lamps, turned off but facing the waters below. He loosens the stand's central fastener with one hand and raises the shaft height with the other until it extends six feet above the deck.

He calls out to George. "Where are they?"

George examines the display at his waist then looks up, scanning the expansive waters before him. He checks the tablet readings again; a cluster of red dots blink at the upper-right of the screen. He extends an arm, pointing northwest off the port side at the boat's ten o'clock position. "There! About three hundred yards and closing."

Jack adjusts the flood lamps, pointing them in the right direction. He flips a switch and illuminates the waters in a wide cone for a hundred yards.

Abbott adjusts the volume control dial of the hydrophonic recorder, watching as the needle indicators spike erratically. He presses a headphone cup firmly against his left ear. "I can hear them!" he yells, then in a whisper, "Unbelievable." The haunting calls of blue whales echo for miles beneath the surface, pulsing with the low frequency tones that suggest an oceanic cardial rhythm. One can more easily feel the language of the massive creatures than hear it.

Jack can just make out the white plumed spray of a whale among the closing pod. Their collective splash breaks the calm of the open ocean sounding like the faint, gentle break of water against a shore. He readies his camera, holding it just inches below his eye line. Another spray erupts from within the closing pod and he snaps a short series of photos.

Abbott estimates the movement of the pod, pointing in the direction of white caps created by the resurfacing whales. The pod nears to fifty yards off the port side, spraying plums of salt water into the air.

Jack makes quick adjustments to his camera and continues snapping off shots as the whales make their way closer, and again submerge twenty yards away.

The surface of the water calms. The only sound is a gentle splash against the hull as the pod passes quietly beneath *The Janet's Doll*, shifting the boat in a gentle roll.

The men look to each other with cautious smiles, silently congratulating themselves for a successful observation.

Jack fiddles with his camera ensuring that everything functioned as expected. The ocean is quiet again.

He switches off the spotlights and starts to the cabin, continuing to scroll through the images on his camera as he moves along the rail.

Whale spray shoots off the immediate port side and *The Janet's Doll* rolls hard to port from the tremendous blow of a passing blue whale. Jack's camera falls from his hand as he grips the rail to keep from going over. The floodlights topple and slide across the deck, crashing into—then under—the rail, falling into the water with little splash. He can see George flailing in the water to his right and scans left to catch a glimpse of Dr. Abbott surfacing for a breath. The boat is pulled sideways by the whale's wake, quickly creating a considerable gap between the two ejected men.

Jack struggles to keep their positions in sight with only the moonlight to illuminate the field. He hears their screams for help, but the sight of the drifting men is lost.

***

Jack scrambles through cabinets grabbing a powerful flashlight. He returns above deck, scanning the waters for any sign of life with a pendulant, conical illumination. He pinpoints the location of Dr. Abbott who struggles to swim forward toward the boat which is drifting away.

He catches the light and waves to Jack with one arm, treading water with the other. He is a hundred feet away, fighting to stay above the surface, gasping for air and spitting the ocean from his mouth.

Jack grabs a life-preserver affixed to the boat with a long, coiled rope and tosses it into the water, coming short of Dr. Abbott's reach.

Abbott splashes frantically toward the preserver, but the gap widens as the ocean current pulls him back.

Jack scans again for George, panning his flashlight from left to right and back again. He spotlights Abbott, now a hundred yards out, staring back motionless, with little energy to keep his head above water. A quick climb up to the cabin and Jack is at the helm, scanning the unfamiliar array of switches, knobs and buttons that comprise the controls. He fumbles with each and manages to turn on the exterior floodlights that cast a powerful beam directly ahead of the bow. With a turn of a key the engine starts.

He peers through the windshield searching again for Dr. Abbott while driving the boat forward and around in a sweeping, clockwise curve attempting to pull up alongside his imperiled friend. A push of the throttle revs the engine hard but the boat gains little distance as the rear of *The Janet's Doll* dips in a sudden motion. Jack looks back, realizing the anchor is still lowered, holding the boat firm to its position. He runs his hand over the dash searching for the proper switch to pull the anchor in. He never imagined a boat this old could be so damn complicated.

Jack pushes the engine again, eyes fixed on the last position of Dr. Abbott. The high-pitched wear of metal stress vibrates through the cabin as the anchor continues to drag behind, raising the bow high above the water.

The Janet's Doll jolts into the air lifting Jack's feet, sending him falling hard to the floor as the boat splashes back onto the water, rolling to the right. The sound of the propellers slicing through whale flesh alerts Jack to the immediate nature of the situation and he jumps up and out of the cabin to see a bleeding behemoth swimming past as if unaffected by the collision. The massive fin of the beast ensnares the anchor line and the boat twist clockwise in its wake, the forward lights now illuminating Dr. Abbott who floats in the distance, eighty yards out. He succumbs to fatigue and slowly sinks below the surface.

Jack considers the situation—then dives into the water.

***

The moonlight makes its way down below the surface, illuminating the gargantuan forms of two dozen blue whales that move past Jack, three and four abreast. He holds his breath, motionless, captivated by the grand spectacle of these living monoliths. The ocean undulates between their graceful movements causing Jack's position to sway softly in alternating directions. He extends a hand as the induced current pushes him to the side. His fingers glide along the smooth surface of cetacean skin, peppered lightly with the rough bump of barnacles which have made a home of the beast.

An intense flash of green light breaks Jack's transient hypnosis and he can just make out the murky form of Dr. Abbott in the distance as it fades, lifeless beneath the surface and descending to the darkness below.

Jack scrambles up, breaking the surface with a deep draw of air as the pod below continues past. The whales spray and take a final breath, submerging until sight of them is lost.

A narrow band of green light trims the entire Bay Area coastline to the east, flashing at points like distant fireworks. The light fades in seconds leaving only the moon and stars to light the ocean.

The Janet's Doll rights herself in the distance, finally freed from entanglement. She comes to a relative halt leaving the life-preserver floating just yards from Jack's position.

He scans the dark searching for any sign of George, treading water in clockwise motion before grabbing for the preserver that conveniently bobs to his side.

LITTLE MAN

The Pacific Northwest. A forest road. Morning.

Edward, mid-twenties, thin mustache, walks along a muddy unpaved road lugging camping gear that looks heavy enough to crush his gaunt five-foot build. Implements of survival dangle about him, clamoring against a rusted iron skillet, well-cleaned of the morning's breakfast. His tie, long since removed, is neatly folded and tucked inside the pocket of his drab woolen suit, indicative of a working-class man of the Wilson era.

The sun shines through a towering canopy of evergreens, casting great shadows across the path. The sky is a blue that can't be found above the calamities of the burgeoning industrial age. Birds and insects make themselves known with sounds that echo throughout the trees.

Edward continues on, the road ahead carved neatly between moss-covered fir, spruce and pine that look to be pillars of an ancient cathedral. He smiles, awed by his surroundings.

A cough escapes him, then another. He stops. The coughing becomes a fit, ailed from deep inside his body. He lets his pack slide carefully off his shoulders and onto the ground, each cough carving flesh from his throat.

He pulls a metal flask from his side and unscrews the cap patiently, waiting a moment for the fit to subside, then drinks.

A brown bear and two cubs meander across the road, not fifty feet away. She pauses only briefly to meet Edward's gaze and sniff at the air. She continues up the embankment to the left, and through the trees.

He follows the kindly beast with his eyes until, slowly, she and the cubs wander away into the wild. He smiles, feeling neither fear nor loneliness.

His cough, but not the pain, subsides. He wipes his lips upon his sleeve and moves on.

**

Eagles circle in the stratosphere. The snow laden peak of a distant mountain can be clearly seen, a hundred miles or more, across valleys of majestic forest.

Edward rests on a felled tree trunk looking out across the wilderness below. The mid-day sun is cooled by a soft breeze. He pulls a brace of dried meat from his pack and eats.

He walks. Hours pass.

The sound of a chainsaw rips through the air. Men call out to each other beyond the tree line. A giant evergreen falls as if in slow motion, unseen, rustling the treetops and shaking the ground.

Edward turns off the muddy road, down a narrow path between the trees.

The forest opens before him. Clear-cut trees lay fallen in an apocalyptic vista that stretches down the valley, patching its way up a distant ridge. Edward is unfazed.

He makes his way down the path, now lined with massive, freshly stacked logs that form a towering wall to one side. The steady thump of machinery grows heavy.

Men call out in the distance. The crackle and tear of a massive pine crashes through the canopy.

He approaches a man wearing the requisite garb of a North American lumberjack; disheveled shirt buttoned to the top, pants held up by suspenders and boots so muddy they seem fused to his legs.

Rain falls hard enough to cleanse the earth.

Introductions go unheard, drowned beneath the din of nature and machinery.

A whistle blows. The men of timber retreat.

***

A campfire burns, encircled by a dozen logs for sitting.

Edward arrives, placing a tin of beans, meat and bread atop a log. He throws a leg over, as if straddling a horse, then the other. He stands, straightening his pants and hops up, sitting on the log, feet dangling inches off the ground. He looks like a child.

He takes up the tin, holding it with one hand to keep it from sliding off the steep incline of his lap.

He digs in, scooping the food, eating.

Across the fire, a man of considerable height steps easily over a log and sits.

The man, tall but thin, with the rugged look of a seasoned woodsman, smiles to Edward and proceeds to eat. He has no problem balancing his tin of food atop his slender, level thighs.

Edward returns a smile and continues to eat.

To his right, another lumberjack, larger than the first in girth, steps easily over Edward's perch, seating himself a few feet to the right. He is a giant, and smiles all the same before commencing his meal.

Yet another, similar in build, joins the fireside trio, then another, until Edward is dwarfed among this congress of Nephilim dressed in plaid cotton, their massive forms accentuated by the flickering up-cast light of the fire.

The man to Edward's right leans in and extends a hand to shake.

"Name's Hal. Where you from?" he asks.

Edward examines the lumberjack's hand. It's huge, inhuman in proportion. He expels a violent coughing fit that lasts until the lumberjack pulls his hand away with a sincere look of concern.

Edward takes up his tin in both hands spinning his body away from the campfire, sliding down from his log perch with unusual grace.

"New York," Edward replies. His Latvian accent is diluted with great effort. He turns to the others with a dry smile. "Please excuse me," he says, and walks away into the darkness.

The circle of burly men follow him with their eyes, then back to each other with an exchange of smiles and shaking heads. They continue their meals to the crackle of damp burning wood.

The night passes. The sun rises.

Great felled trees, eight feet in diameter and nearly two-hundred long, lie strewn across the embankment for a hundred yards in every direction. Forty men are scattered, some chopping branches from the fallen trees with axes, others positioning timber with heavy iron poles.

Edward walks with another across the embankment.

The man is slender and feeble-looking, unlike the others, yet still a foot taller than Edward. His clothes are worn and over-sized, but appropriate enough for the heavy labor of logging. He seems the happy sort, waving greetings to fellow loggers as they pass. The burliest push and pull at two-man saws cutting felled trees in half. They stop to return the man's greeting with a "Mornin', Arty!"

"Them's buckers," Arty says, motioning to the sawing men. "They cut the timber down to smaller pieces that the yarding can handle."

Rugged men fasten steel cables around tree stumps boxed around an immense standing tree, branches hacked away and topped-off.

"These fellas here are settin' up the yarding and guy-lines, what's used to drag timber from the field to that-there spar-tree."

The rugged men pull the steel lines taut, forming what looks like the skeleton of a hundred-foot-tall tent.

The camp foreman turns to greet Arty and Edward as they approach, removing his leather gloves to extend a hand.

Edward coughs, eyeing the man's large hand.

The burly man holds back a laugh.

"This ain't a place for sickly fellas," the foreman says. His hand still extended in greeting.

Edward takes the foreman's hand and shakes, straightening his posture in a gesture of fitness.

"Just a bit of dust, is all," he says, mimicking the country speak.

Arty puts a firm hand on Edward's shoulder.

"Ed here's fit as a fiddle. And he's aimin' to get started."

Edward glimpses uncomfortably at the hand on his should then to back to the foreman.

"I can do the work of any man here."

Several men within earshot halt their labors and turn, amused at the bold statement of this little man. Chuckles can be heard.

Edward eyes stay on the foreman's.

Arty removes his hand from Edward's shoulder, embarrassed.

Again, the foreman holds back a laugh. "We'll see, little man." He puts his gloves back on with a smile and glimpse to Arty for reaction.

"So then," he continues, "are you a *donkey*?" He looks back to his men who are leaning against some sort of steam powered machine. "Or are you a *bull*?

The men in the rear snicker until the foreman waves them off.

Arty bites a lip, unseen by Edward who looks about, choosing his words.

"I am certainly no donkey," he replies.

The men in the rear chuckle, shake heads, then return to their business.

"Right you are," the foreman says. "Bull it is." He pats Edward hard on the arm. "Arty, get our friend acquainted with his new job."

Arty points Edwards to the bulky steam driven machine off to the side.

"That there's a steam engine we use to pull the timber on steel lines from one place to another place. It's called a donkey. This here donkey's named Jenny." He motions to the men standing around the steam engine.

Edward looks fascinated by the machinery. It's been a few years since he's worked in a camp and his familiarity with logging doesn't include this modern technology.

"These fine gentlemen are called donkey-punchers. It's their job to keep Jenny purring like a kitten. They work the levers, hauling loads a hundred men can't budge." He picks up an empty tin bucket from the side of the path, handing it to Edward, who examines it, now expecting the worst.

"The bull-cook does all the ..." Arty considers his words.

Hal at the donkey fills in the blank. "Woman's work."

"He gathers water for the boys," Arty continues. "Makes the beds. This and that sort of business."

"And cleans the latrines," another man adds.

Arty gives the man a disapproving look.

"Latrines? You mean I have to clean the toilets?"

Arty looks down at the bucket in Edward's hand.

"Well, no, Ed. I wouldn't go quite so far as to call them *toilets*."

He gestures for Edward to continue walking. "Don't fret, though. Everyone starts out as bulls when they first get here. We'll get you in the field soon enough."

They move on through the field of felled trees and tin buckets.

"Now, there goes an odd little guy," one man tells another.

***

The camp is empty if not for Edward chopping firewood over a tree stump. He swings the axe high and lets gravity do the rest, splitting the log like a seasoned woodsman. He takes one of the cleaved halves, then the other, pitching them onto a sizeable pile of what looks to be hundreds of split logs.

Hal, dirty and perspiring from the field, approaches as Edward readies another log on the stump. He eyes the pile of firewood as he comes near.

"Shoot, brother! That is a fine job you're doin'!" He is panting from the walk up.

Edward raises the axe, then splits. He catches a breath, wiping the sweat from his brow.

"A good man is never idle," he says in a huff.

Hal looks a little bewildered. "Sure enough. A man's gotta keep movin'. But look there."

He points to a location behind the half-dozen makeshift housing shacks, where stands a wall of considerable mass made entirely of cut and neatly stacked cords of wood.

"If it's one thing we got plenty of in this camp, it's firewood."

Edward lets out a quiet series of coughs, then takes up the split wood and tosses them onto his pile.

Wiping his brow, Hal continues. "If you can find time in your busy schedule, Boss-man wants you to fetch some water for the ox."

***

The sun shines bright from between the occasional clouds.

A great log, eight-foot-wide and one-hundred fifty feet long, is being slowly dragged along the ground at the end of a steel cable. The cable stretches up to the top of a massive spar-tree where it weaves through pulleys and back down to a steam donkey, its piston engine thumping and bellowing steam.

Edward carries two large buckets of water, dangling from a wooden pole laid across his shoulders.

A man in the distance cries "WHOA!" The donkey-punchers pull levers.

The great log is stopped near the base of the spar-tree, suspended above of a vast cold deck of other such sizeable timbers, stacked for relocation.

One end of the great log hangs high in the air, dangling from the steel cable.

Edward looks up, away from the activity, staring at the sky.

The two oxen to his side dip muzzles into the buckets and drink.

He lowers the buckets to the ground, his gaze fixed up to a distant point.

Hal catches Edward staring up at the sky and follows his line of sight.

The foreman approaches. He too follows Edward's line of sight, beyond the commotion of work and up. Clouds move slowly in, closing around an otherwise empty sky. Hal catches the foreman's gaze and they smile as if sharing a joke.

"I'll get more water straight away, sir," Edward says.

"Don't bother. That'll do for now."

"Yes, sir. I'll get back to the camp then."

"Nah, the camp can wait. What I need is another bucker."

"Bucker, sir?"

"Yeah, I need that raw timber into smaller pieces. Can you handle that?"

The oxen next to Edward are led away by a worker, toward the spar-tree in the distance.

Men down the hillside work at a two-man saw, cutting a large tree in half. Another wields a great double-blade axe, striking chunks of wood from a felled spruce.

"I can. Thank you."

"Yeah, right then."

He motions down the hillside toward the men wielding the two-man saw.

"Go talk to Deon. He'll fix you up with the gear and show you—"

With a CRACK! the pulley atop the spar-tree breaks free. The great log falls hard. The ground beneath the mammoth pile of timber gives way. Ground and logs become an unstoppable force, flowing downhill in a fifty-yard-wide landslide. Men dash to the clear, yelling to each other to run. The cable fixed to the great log goes taut ripping the iron steam donkey from its place, thrown into the air like a toy.

A dozen oxen are swept away beneath the tide of bloody soil and timber. The crew watches helplessly as a week of hard labor settles, a hundred yards away, at the bottom of the slope.

***

The embankment, once a scene of productivity, is a patch of barren dirt. The spar-tree stands unattended near the top of the inclination, its pulley system and cables torn from their mounts. Bodies of oxen lay mutilated in the field. A worker leads two horses on foot. They struggle to tow a small log of timber up the hill. He tugs hard on the reigns to move them forward.

The horses rear up and stop, neighing with exhaustion.

Edward, examining the mangled block and pulley system, stops and takes notice.

The foreman waves the worker to stop, approaching at a hurry.

"Hold up!" the foreman shouts.

The horses pant and step back to loosen the lines that connect them to the timber load. The foreman takes the reins from the worker's hand and pats a horse on the muzzle.

"That's all for now. They won't be any more good tonight," he says, then signals with a yanking motion to a man in the distance.

A loud whistle blows. The sun is setting over a distant ridge.

Dozens of men stop their feeble attempts to right the disaster and make their way, exhausted and hungry, to the main dirt path where the foreman awaits.

Edward removes his gloves and approaches Hal.

"There's a thousand tons of fresh-cut timber piled at the bottom of this hill, bellow a thousand tons of dirt," Hal says.

Tired men close in from all directions, silhouetted against an orange sky. The foreman steps onto a tree stump and addresses the men who are gathering around him, hoping for guidance.

"It was worth a try, fellas," the foreman starts. "But without a donkey and ox team to haul the timber back up the hill, we're just stuck in the mud. We'll keep fellin', but it'll be a week at least till we get some new gear."

He steps down from the stump.

"Go on back to camp and get some grub. We'll start back up in the mornin'."

"And under all that dirt and timber, there's my paycheck," Hal grumbles to no one in particular.

***

It's dark inside the wooden quarters, housing twenty bed bunks, stacked two high, ten to a side. The men lie sleeping under cotton sheets after a grueling day's work. The moonlight enters through the two widows near the door. In the far corner, a single candle illuminates a bottom bunk.

Edward sits propped up, wearing neatly pressed clothes he would never sleep in. With a worn-down pencil in his right hand he turns the pages of a leather-bound journal, stopping at a booked-marked page. The photo is a young woman, possibly just a teen. She is unassuming, with the typical stern look of someone trying to keep still during the long process of having their picture taken. He places the photograph on the bed and begins to write. Arty drops his hands then head down from the bunk above, hanging upside-down. The flickering light illuminates the grime on his face from a day of hard labor, too tired to wash.

Edward doesn't seem to notice, continuing to write, the photograph at his side.

Arty reaches down and picks up the photograph.

"Who's this?" he asks.

Edward takes the photograph from Arty's hand and fondly re-examines it.

"My sweet sixteen," Edward replies.

"She your wife?"

"No. Not yet."

Someone in an adjacent bunk rolls over and grumbles, perturbed.

"Well, why don't you give her a kiss goodnight so I can get some sleep?"

Edward closes his journal, taking it with him as he steps outside, candle in hand.

***

The forest can't be seen beyond ten feet. The rest is blackness. He sits down at a large wooden table, setting the candle down and opening his journal.

Edward removes the picture of his "Sweet Sixteen" and sets it down, admiring it as he always does, drawing inspiration from the visage of his muse. He pulls the pencil from a shirt pocket and resumes his writing.

Hidden all around, crickets scratch out a chorus. A slight breeze rustles the forest canopy. The candle flame flickers.

Edward, distracted, looks deeply into the darkness. The silhouettes of trees sway against a starlit sky.

The candle flame goes out.

Edward's own body is barely visible as he pats pockets for the matches he left in the shack. He can see the smoldering red embers of the night's earlier fire dwindling in the distance near the shack. He looks up, his attention drawn to something through the tree-line. Beyond the black shapes of fir and pine can be seen, what looks to be, the light of a lantern moving slowly between the trunks of the trees, fifty yards away. He stands, tracking the ghostly glow as he steps back and over the bench, stuffing the journal into his back pocket.

He walks onward, toward the light, into the darkness.

***

A central wood stove warms the small, single room cabin. The foreman sits at the edge of the bed, pulling on his boots, still covered in mud. He takes a sip of coffee from a tin on the nightstand.

A hard knock at the door, then it opens from outside. Arty shows himself in.

"Just because you knock doesn't mean you can come in."

"Sorry, boss. You're gonna wanna see this."

***

A mammoth stack of felled timber lies surrounding the base of the spar-tree. A hundred trees, some eight feet wide and two-hundred feet long, make a wall nearly fifty feet high and just as deep. The foreman examines the anomaly, scratching his head. Dozens of workers gander as others walk around the timber stack in wonder.

"That's gotta be about a thousand tons of timber," Arty estimates.

"Well, where the hell'd it come from?"

Arty points loosely down the hill to where yesterday's landslide deposited the week's worth of felled trees.

"From the bottom of the slope, I reckon. But don't ask me how."

They can see what's left of the steam-driven pulley, stuck half-deep in mud and scattered in pieces about two-hundred yards off at the base of the hill.

"With the donkey broke?"

"Seems so," Arty replies.

"And how the hell'd they get stacked without the spar cables?"

They look up to the top of the spar-tree where the pulley was violently dislodged.

"Dead oxen to boot."

The foreman shakes his head slowly. He pulls a pair of leather working gloves from his back pocket, slapping them against his leg as if to beat the dust. "Well, I'll be goddamned."

***

Shadows are cast far by the morning sun.

Edward walks along a lonely dirt road flanked by virgin pastures and the occasional pond, the Cascade mountain range behind him in the distance. The implements of a vagabond dangle from his haversack. He looks over his shoulder to see a Ford Model T approaching, its narrow wheels weaving clumsily through hardened carriage grooves.

He steps to the side, watching as the Ford passes from behind. It comes to a wobbling halt several yards up, its twenty-horsepower engine idling with the distinctive thump of early American industry.

Edward waits, not to assume an invitation, his gear weighing heavy on his shoulder.

The passenger door of the Model T swings open.

MEI

She works her way through the crowd, her baby girl nestled to her back in a colorful makeshift sling, half asleep, half awake. A hundred yards down at the base of the hill, an open-air movie is playing on the silver screen before an ocean of townsfolk. Most sit on the grass in quiet immersion as she crouches past, while dramatized sounds of European battles echo up the valley.

Masses have gathered from across the Chinese county of Wuyuan to enjoy a rare showing of a foreign film, furnished by the maternal provincial government of Jiangxi. Mei estimates that there must be three thousand in attendance with more trickling in every minute, bottle-necked at the few ticket tables where they pay the pittance fee of two jiao. On this night it's a classic Romanian film espousing the virtues of socialist reformation, dub poorly in Mandarin and guaranteed to end in a glorious victory. It doesn't matter that the movie started twenty minutes before she arrived. It doesn't matter that she can hardly hear the audio. It doesn't even matter that she speaks only English and Cantonese, which she teaches to foreigners in Hong Kong. Tonight is the only opportunity she'll have to decompress and enjoy the provincial surroundings before being shuttled in the morning to the capital of Nanchang for a direct flight back to her metropolitan island home. She finds an open spot and sits on the grass, taking her baby from the sling and coddling her against a bare shoulder.

Mei looks around, admiring the general air of consideration that blankets the gathering. Crowds are never this quiet in Hong Kong, she thinks. The eastern world has always had a greater appreciation for the mundane, making more out off less. Movie goers in Hong Kong tend to become rowdy with frustration. She's seen people throw food at the screens in Hong Kong, especially if the context is overtly socialist.

An elderly man to Mei's left greets her with a quiet smile which she returns in kind, turning the baby slightly in his direction to show her off. He seems struck by Mei's beauty. She is thirty-five, but few would guess. She has lived a soft life and reminds herself of this daily. Hardship is merely a concept that her family tries to appreciate, but has never known. Her baby girl wriggles about and closes her eyes, letting sleep take hold. Mei combs the baby's thin black hair with her finger tips until she turns her tiny head to one side and settles in. The old man points to the baby and gives what sounds to Mei like kind words in the local dialect. She bows her head and gives a conciliatory smile, not understanding what was said, only knowing his tone is a gentle sign of acceptance. They both turn back to the silver screen below.

Grenades exploded. Machinegun fire rings out. Romanian soldiers rush a hill of some apparent consequence. Their defunct flag, of an era gone by, held high above their shoulders as they battle their western foes from bunker to bunker.

A girl of twelve moves through the crowd selling dumplings and rice balls from a bamboo tray. Her mother works the far end pouring refreshments into paper cups, handing them to grateful patrons on the grass. Mei stretches her neck above the crowed to catch a glimpse of the beverages that might be available if she waits long enough. A thirst has taken hold of her. It's a warm summer night and, as usual, the humidity in Zhangpo is uncomfortably high. Mei looks around and back over her shoulder. The wandering vendor seems a lifetime away and the refreshment stands are fifty yards back, up the hill and through the hushed crowd from where she entered. She should have considered this sooner, but no matter. If she moved now she would certainly lose her spot. Her baby's cheek is warm against her skin. A light perspiration glistens on her shoulders. She notices that she is practically the only person not wearing long sleeves. Socialists must be cold blooded. She should have brought a fan.

The flag is hoisted high atop a desolate hill, soldiers raising their rifles in salute. Victory has come to the people's army! Gunfire spits out and cheers yelled with glee. The western dog is defeated. Long live the socialist brigade! Long live Romania!

A few yards ahead a man stretches out his arm pointing to the western sky. The others around him begin to rustle, turning with whispers to their neighbors and pointing in kind to the night. A mumble of voices rolls up the hill. Mei looks up and to her left.

Two lights hover, like bright stars far above the tops of trees in the distance. Mei's baby moans sweetly and turns her head in slumber. One light seems to grow and elongate its shape. The smaller begins to slowly pulsate.

Soldiers of the Motherland, battered but victorious, start the long journey home. They help their wounded heroes stand high, shoulder to shoulder and proud to the last. They cover their dead in the flags of their country and sing a quiet song of war.

A collective murmur rolls over the crowd, hundreds now pointing and peering up to the peculiar lights in the sky, nudging the fellows at their sides to draw their attention from the film.

Fireworks detonate above an enthusiastic populous. The people line the streets cheering as their victorious soldiers march past, flags held high, boots polished and buffed. The Motherland is whole again. Her citizens rejoice!

People get to their feet. A commotion envelopes the crowd. Mei pushes herself up with one arm, standing to get a better view while holding her baby snug to her shoulder. The smaller light turns from white to green, pulsating slowly. The larger light seems to rotate and change its oblong form. Both objects pulsate in sync, alternating color from white to green to orange then back again. The crowd begins to move. Onlookers gather their things and make their way back toward the gate. Mass anxiety sets in.

The objects descend slowly then move forward, toward the crowd. A scream is heard and becomes infectious.

Confetti pours down upon the conquering heroes. Women raise their children, shouting their gratitude. Orchestral horns trumpet their song of victory and a hearty chorus bids them well.

A crushing mass of people turn and push toward the top of the hill, back toward the entry of the outdoor theater and away from the approaching lights. Waves of limbs and muscle wash over those that hadn't made it to their feet. Pleas for help are smothered in the din. Those unbalanced by the confusion are trampled by the persistent throw.

Mei stands, baby held tight against her breast, watching as the strange lights drop altitude and move slowly toward the frenzy. The mob rushes past with bruising distress, yet she holds her ground, oblivious to the assault. Her skin is showered in colors from above. Her eyes reflect the universe.

Ever silent, Mei's baby girl watches these marvels approach with innocent wonder.

SHOTGUN SUMMER

Celestial Paradigms. Servonomicon. The Great Freeze. Macrovores and Hermaphronoids. Liquid shirts with upturned collars and drugs that make your slippers taste like pie. The planet roils from the Love Laws and pukes terra-trash onto the farthest districts of the Zone. The new-pubescent youth spit on encapsulated health and board their buggies to the disaffected center of the universe—Dolce's Café, *Earth*.

The block is littered with teenage deviants, tattooed rebels from space defending their plot against the forces of Solar-class congeniality. I'd start a war if it weren't so fuckin' hot in these boots.

But, thank God for sundown.

I've been sitting on this sidewalk for three hours, my back against the storefront, sipping lukewarm cola and extolling the virtues of the Arabica bean to my bloodshot companions. My feet drip inside my calf-high motor-boots;

my Mohawk hangs low like a paraffin sundial. Maybe it's the way the air settles and stagnates between the maze of mega-sprawling shopping-plexes and cloud-piercing monuments to the all-consuming oligarchy, but July always seems hotter downtown.

Dolce's serves the usual boiling assortment of caffeinated consumables, but it has to be ninety-eight degrees outside and I haven't gotten around to removing my leather jacket. Colony towns are climate controlled—but Earth's? The cheap bastards. I am absolutely on fire, but I'm not about to lose my cool. I wouldn't consider a wardrobe change until I feel the bitter sting of sweat in my eyes.

Baby Bad Babies and the Jehovah's Vandals hit the free-radio airwaves and kids from across the system flock to the scene like shrapnel to a B-17. Somebody inside is playing Circle Jerks covers on a wooden guitar. Amazing. It's like a punk rock Renaissance Fair. Rebellion's in the air and it feels like wet leather.

Tim is a few feet away trying to extort credits off some poor soul who probably wandered too far from his mansion in the outer-sect. He turns and catches my gaze, gritting his teeth with a simulated madness.

"What're you looking at, freak?" he scowls, followed by a discreet wink and his signature grin that always makes my skin crawl.

"I really need to change my socks," I tell him, furrowing my brow and trying not to laugh; he's got this kid's collar in a grip with one hand and jabbing at his gut with the other— palm up— half expecting doubloons to spill out of him like a Japanese pachinko machine.

Tim is a dick, my best friend, and my roommate, but saying that he shares the rent with me would be a very loose assessment. He smells like death and sports a self-inflicted scar that frames his left eye and trails down to his cheek—a question mark with only one right answer. It's disturbing to look at and probably the only reason I let him hang out with me. The fact that nobody likes Tim only adds to his mystique.

But I wasn't kidding about my socks. My boots are a jungle and the forecast is moist. So let it be said that no advancements in space-age textile development can supplant the age-old tactile comfort of a minty-fresh pair of common cotton socks.

Alicia is shy, beautiful and 'Off World'. I'd fallen for her the day she walked into my Exo-Language class, mid-semester, wearing a fashionable overcoat with a matching hue of cherry-red lipstick. She'd moved to my town from Arsia Mons or some such alien land, looking like an electric angel with her off-kilter hair and soap bar skin. And there she stands, ordering her usual large cola with ice, not pretending to not notice me. Ahhhhh, yeah ... young love. There's nothing worse, and it's the only reason I'd wait here, melting in the summer sun, hoping for the opportunity to embarrass myself with a solid show of desperation. I'll dazzle her with my charm, launching into a conversation that's been burning a hole in my nut for the past six months: "Hey there, beautiful, I'm Blik ... Oh, you already know my name?.. Cool ... Hey, I wanted to ask you if ... Yes? What? Outside your window? When? Last night? No, that wasn't me."

She's currently being propositioned by Akio Oshiro, a self-proclaimed playboy (and utter razzbot) from the outer-sect, but I'm sure her sweet giggles and generous smiles are just some feminine ploy to lead bonks like him to a gruesome end. Psycho-femmes I can handle, but sexual statistics? Well, they carry baggage.

9PM. Still hot. Still hanging out in front of Dolce's waiting for something hip to go down. Probably too late now to take off my jacket. I've already made it this far, it just wouldn't make any sense. Even among the wayward youth there are expectations. We rebel against our parents. We rebel against our posh towns. We definitely rebel against those tuggin' prep kids from Ceres Colony IV and we'd be damned if we're gonna let the weather call the shots. The jacket stays on. I give the bird to some Yupper walking by, my lungs struggling to pull in air.

Nestor pretends to trip over my legs and lands harder than he poorly planned. He's one of those guys that'll turn his intended folly into a piss-rage just to spare himself a harmless chiding, so I cut him off before he can launch a formal complaint.

"If you wore a shirt every once in a while you wouldn't scab your nipples so much," I point out, watching him brush the pebbles off his bare chest.

"Do you even have nipples, Blik? I thought they melted away with your mommy's sweet kisses."

He's never seen me without a shirt on, and I don't think that's even possible.

"Jokes are no substitute for a protective layer of synthesized fabric," I argue, rubbing my chest in a mock sensuality that lasts just long enough to make him feel uncomfortable. I pinch at my jacket to ply the T-shirt from my damp skin, making the sucking sound of cellophane being peeled off a warm Christmas ham.

He sidles next to me, straddling the smooth composite deck of his MagSlide, bobbing up and down until his weight equilibrates on its magnetically induced cushion of air. I've never had the nerve to traverse the Zone on a floating plank of plastic death, but damn if this concrete slab beneath my ass isn't counseling me to reassess its value.

"We're all heading up to Devil's Point tonight to check out the lunar eclipse," he says, digging about in a sort of refrigerated fanny-pack on his lap. "You should come."

"Who's we?" I'd consider pouring sand down my boots if the option would present itself. My butt has gone numb and I'm shifting from cheek to cheek.

Nestor finds his inhaler and takes a hit.

"Azure'll be there," he adds.

She's Nestor's gal—or sister—or both. They look like twins with their long, tight curls and I'm sure I've seen them kiss.

"and Jackson ..."

His name isn't really 'Jackson', it's Alvin Mellish. The origin of his moniker escapes me, but he's one of Nestor's cronies and he shares the same aversion to practical outerwear.

"You know *Snow* will definitely be there ..."

I'm not going to admit that I have no idea who 'Snow' is. It could be some platinum blonde babe from a neighboring sect or it could be an albino with a penchant for mountaineering. You never know from nicknames. But probably this is some sort of illicit drug reference by the way Nestor's grinning at me.

"and Super-Frank ..."

Frank is *the show*, I'll give you that. One man band. In action, he's a treat to behold.

"and Bob ..."

Which one?

"and Alicia ..."

Bingo. "I'll be there." But not before I change my socks. Who knew that feet had so many glands?

"and her little brother."

Good Lord, why?

Nestor hops on his board and pushes off, leaving behind a patch of wet on the wall.

"And don't bring that idiot Tim!" he shouts, flipping innumerable gestures in Tim's direction.

Tim turns, greeting Nestor with a choice gesture of his own, holding tight to a handful of credits he's just purloined.

***

10PM AND I'VE GOT SWAMPFOOT.

My socks are saturated with sweat and they've worked their way down, inexorably, to the front of my boots. I feel the uneasy sensation of the ocean between my toes.

Main Street runs a straight shot from the café to my lowly domicile and I'm halfway home. Tim has removed his jacket and slung it over his shoulder, trying to look cool, but I know better - nobody looks cool when they're perspiring. I'm pretty sure he can hear the moisture in my boots make a squishing sound with every step I take, but looking at him puts me right at ease. He looks ridiculous. I'm a close second, but Tim really looks fuckin' ridiculous.

And I forgot about the hill. A billion years of geological upheaval stuck a steep grade between me and my pad and I'm about to pass out. I'm seconds from parking my ass on the sidewalk and removing my socks, but I'm already riding that fine line between looking punk rock and looking homeless and nuts. My clothes are dirty, I'm sweating and my hair is pasted to my face. Socks are all I have left of humanity so I tell Tim he looks absurd and push on.

***

10-SOMETHING PM.

We're rounding the corner and there's a police cruiser pulling up to my hovel. Tim wants to dash, but I tug at his leash and tell him to stay. This is probably his doing anyway. There are any number of reasons for metro law to bust down my door, but to simply knock? Well, now that gives one pause.

Tim looks guilty, but he only has two looks to choose from so I don't even bother to ask. I'm just a hundred feet away from a fresh pair of paw liners, but cops trump comfort and I'm not about to miss my chance at love.

Some goiter in a convertible Falcon Devastator slides his floating alloy beast to a daft halt, cutting us off as we turn to make our retreat. He revs his engine, making the sound of a humming bird at a gunnery range.

"I've been looking for you everywhere," the driver says. "Get in."

The door to the Devastator eases open as if controlled by telekinesis. An array of multi-colored dashboard indicators pop and blink with seizure inducing regularity. His face comes clear from under a white-brimmed pimp cap and I realize I know who this rapscallion is.

"No time to reminisce, Nance." I tell him. "I'm on a mission of love."

I throw a few mock punches at the air and a karate kick in his general direction. Moisture sloshes about in my boot and I regret my impromptu display of bravado.

"Not you, strawberry," Nance replies. "Tim."

Nance's line of sight tells me he's keen to the cops and in a hurry to scuttle.

Tim bounces into the front seat, grinning back at me like he's just been crowned the King of All Things Crazy. It's rare he gets to show me up and I can't help but feel a sick sense of pride. He's like a horny, retarded brother with a skill set so limited I loath to wonder what Nance could possibly ever want with him.

"Are you getting in or what?" Nance blasts, looking from me to Tim who is pushing dashboard buttons at random, fascinated by the pretty, pretty lights. "The monkey needs its handler."

It's a couple more hours before Earth's umbra blankets the Moon, aligning the celestial bodies in syzygy, so I jump in the backseat and take a chance. When you hang out with minor criminals adventure is never far off, and I could really use a ride to the nearest retail bargain shack.

***

It's no big secret that universities and intelligence communities only recruit those wretched few whose parents didn't have the means (or the common sense) to fit their newborns with the latest in in-ware augmentation. Reason being, it's been understood for generations that these devices, implanted directly into the brain, stunt your cognitive abilities by providing you with a feed of instantaneously accessible data, thus minimizing the necessary cerebral exercise required to calculate mathematics, general problem-solve or recall information. Who invented Velcro? Beats me. What is the ratio of septic systems-to-Buddhist temples in Kathmandu? Hell if I know. What's fifteen times nine? Give me a minute and something to write on and I'll let you know, but I certainly can't just spew the answers to these kinds of questions like most people can. Why? Because I haven't been hardwired to the grid like ninety-nine-point-nine percent of the population.

My mother, raised in a commune by paranoid subversives, was unnaturally wary of neural implants and my father (whoever he might be) took a permanent leave of absence before I saw the light of day. I missed out on the crucial first year of infancy when the brain is malleable enough to accept that sort of artificial material without eventually encasing it in a nasty malignant tumor. But given that all my friends are both *plugged-in* and complete morons, I can confidently consider myself lucky to be living on the outs.

The upshot to being an unplugged pariah is, when the neuro-grid finally goes down—and it certainly will—I'll be the only guy left who can recall his girlfriend's address or reheat a frozen slice of pizza without calling in for technical support. So why do the masses buy into the cyclic dependence of virtual intelligence? For the same reason gentiles get circumcised: it's an easy alternative to washing your penis.

In my humble opinion, we are well-into the final downward spiral of mankind, when me and the rest of the meek shall most certainly inherit a giant fuckin' mess.

Anyways, the landscape is zipping by as we cruise the Devastator down a lonely tract in the mid-belt span and Tim is glaring back at me from the front seat, razzing at the fact that I've been talking to myself ever since we skipped the Zone.

***

"We're not stopping, Blik, so if you say one more thing about your goddamn socks I'm gonna degauss your ass! Just sit back and enjoy the ride," Nance yells, eyeballing me hard through the rearview.

"You'd have to stop to kick my ass, and where exactly are you taking us anyways?"

I'm sensing this foray get beleaguered so I'm questioning my decision to get in the car.

Tim turns to chime in with, "Take 'em off and hang 'em from the back. They'll air dry in a few minutes then you can stop whining."

I'm not whining. My tone is low, slow and calculated. I never whine—ever—but Tim's suggestion is so elegant in its simplicity I'm almost embarrassed he thought of it first.

"Pure genius," I shout, giving credit where it's due and grabbing for my boot buckles.

Nance spins his head around so fast we swerve into oncoming traffic.

"Keep your socks on, strawberry. You're not mucking up my Devastator with your mangy shrimp-slips," he barks, turning forward in time to avoid barreling us off the express. "Besides, we're almost there."

We steer off the main, cruising up a dilapidated stretch of off-grid road.

"My crew got cold and I need a crazy-looking fool like Tim to back me up," he explains.

Tim is a really nice guy if you don't have anything worth taking. He doesn't kill me because I treat him better than his mother, and I let him squat at my flat because my building doesn't allow for pets. It's a symbiotic compromise to a meaningful relationship.

Tim pops in his seat, jerking like a sugar-high toddler with a diaper full of sweets.

"Who do I get to hurt?"

"That's the spirit, Tim!"

Nance throws a fist in the air, grinning, but acutely aware of Tim's metal studded jacket threatening to scratch against the Devastator's custom, red leatherette upholstery.

I know Tim well enough to know that he prefers to reserve his violence for special occasions, so I'm hoping that his enthusiasm here is just for show. I'm wondering just how much *joy* I'm going to get out of this *ride* and my brain is parsing overtime, constructing a con to get me out of this floating boat and into a dry pair of woven hoses.

"This chump from the Out's," Nance starts. "He's got something to drop, but the bastard's playing coy. Now listen up 'cause I'll only tell you once. This info dies with us. Super hush-hush."

He dogs us, waiting for a sign of understanding, but settles for a look of impatience.

"His name's Akio Oshiro," he continues, "and he tells me ... dug up ... alien ... black cube ... fish market ... space shield ... lunar eclipse ... bikini party. Hey asshole, are you listening to me?"

Akio Oshiro. His name falls from my gullet like bitter pharmacon. He's the razz that's been playing on Alicia's sweet, sweet affections thus shanking my amorous devices. This lustful lady-killer must be stopped before civilization or my libido takes a decisive hit.

Nance goes on with, "Tim, I need you to put on your meanest face."

Tim glares back, locking his jaw and curling up his lips, revealing a medieval mess of yellowish choppers. He growls fiercely, spittle spraying asunder and dripping down his boney chin. It's disturbing as hell and a look only his handler could love.

"Jesus Christ," Nance grumbles. "Let's tone that down a bit."

"What about me?" I ask as we pull up to a building that looks like an abandoned relic from a time when shit moved on wheels.

"You watch the car," Nance replies, opening the door and walking away, with Tim following close behind.

I let out something between a sigh and a grunt as they disappear into the shadow of the building.

***

The moon is still full—its luminous, yellow face not yet contaminated by the impending umbrage of Earth. I'm hoping that means the party on Devil's Point hasn't started, because my plan to win the girl rather involves me being present when it happens.

A false star twinkles high above the horizon with the distinctive blue cast of a colony-cluster orbiting the sun somewhere between Mars and Ceres. Or is it Saturn and Uranus? It doesn't matter. It's yet another reminder that affluence courts lunacy and lunacy is king. Why anyone would choose to leave behind the wondrous stench of organic firma in exchange for a promise of the sterilized longevity of space is far beyond my understanding. Who wants to live for two-hundred years in a pressurized floating fishbowl? Well, apparently the answer is a shit-ton of people do and I say good riddance to them all. That's more Dim-Sum for me, my friends. Purified air and folic reductive chem-baths can never replace the existential aromas that waft from the kitchens of the neighborhood Cantonese Pick-N-Fry. I spit on manufactured longevity and the boredom it cultivates. Give me fireworks. I want the bang.

Take for example, Tim and Nance—Two guys who don't give a clown's balls about tomorrow, much less a hundred years from now—and the sight of them dragging an unconscious Japanese man toward me now is simply a granular sampling of their collective *joie de vivre*.

"Get off the hood, strawberry, and open the trunk."

Considering Nance is holding a comatose man in his hands, I sit up, jump down and—

"How do you open the trunk?"

"You're kidding me," Nance snaps. "It's a trunk. You just open it, dumb-dumb."

"Those are just words. What I need is a lever or button or a spell of some kind."

"Driver's side. Button. Pictograph of a trunk on it," he directs, watching me play daft, shrugging my shoulders like the act of walking around to the driver's side and pushing a button is beyond my comprehension.

He cries, "Forget it!" and lets go of Akio's arm, who slumps over; his other arm held up limply by Tim.

"Never ask the unplugged to do a man's job!"

Tim lets go and Akio drops like a doll to the dirt.

Nance finger-draws an invisible symbol onto the palm of his left hand until a beep is heard and the trunk pops open, like old magic.

"Gimme your socks," Nance demands.

"No," I say, instinctively turning to Tim. "What the hell did you do to him?" shoots out of me with a tone of such concern I feel a little embarrassed. I've already decided that this reality isn't exactly what I bargained for when I imagined taking Akio out of the picture, so playing the upright citizen here may go a long way to keep me from spending the rest of my life behind bars with these two numbskulls. I'm definitely not helping them put an Asian narcoleptic in the trunk, and I'm sure as shit not giving anybody my socks.

"Nothing," Tim replies, with a look so disappointed I just have to believe him. "I didn't do anything!" He's all puppy-eyed and pouty now, like the day he lost his favorite knife. Little brings him down like the missed opportunity to hit somebody.

"We didn't touch him," Nance adds, throwing a suspicious-looking satchel into the trunk of the Devastator. He wasn't carrying this on his way to the building so I can only assume it belongs to Akio. "He just fainted or something when we walked through the door. Now give me your damn socks."

"No," I repeat, sneaking a peek at the satchel in the trunk, then back down at Akio who is lying unconscious, nose to the ground, at their feet. "I don't know what you're up to, but I'm gonna need these socks for the long walk home."

"We need to tie him up, strawberry."

"So find some rope."

We turn our heads, collectively looking about in the dark void around this empty lot. North of us is downtown Zone, the inner-most section from whence we came. Between here and the inner-sect is about five miles of broken plots of derelict housing projects, one of which I lived in before the enforcement of Consolidation. To the south is pretty much the same deal. But east of downtown is the opulent land of milk and money, commonly known to us urban denizens as the 'Outer-Sect'. This is where the affluent have manufactured their personal utopia and electronically walled-out the working-class riff-raff. This is where the houses *aren't* stacked on top of each other and compressed into barely-habitable cubes with roommates who don't pay the rent. And this outer section of the Zone is where Akio and his soul-sucking, love-napping ilk dwell.

So, summing up the situation, it's pretty obvious we aren't going to find any rope.

I would tell Nance to use his own socks but I can see he's wearing the short ankle-type which are fine for keeping your shrimps warm, but useless for binding limbs.

"You can use Tim's socks," I suggest, assuming they're more suitable to the task given the gratuitously high throat of his ass-kicking boots.

"I'm not wearing any," he replies.

Nance and I look at him. Sweat has matted his tuft of ginger hair and is dripping off his brow. His shirt, like mine, is pasted to his skin. All the moisture from this putrid, sultry night must be collecting deep inside his multi-buckled, paramilitary, double-tough, bull leather, steel-toed, knee-high, motor-boots.

"Tim," I start, pausing to restrain my reaction, "that is absolutely disgusting."

Nance agrees. Akio would agree if he were conscious. Even Tim agrees, but he's giving me that twentieth-century, impoverished child of despair look, so I re-swallow my lunch and block the thought.

Something beeps from inside the seriously-suspicious-looking satchel in the open trunk, but Nance calls my attention before I can open my mouth.

"Once again, Blik," he begins, "you've been an absolutely useless pain in the ass."

I counter with "I aim to please," and consider the situation while Tim helps Nance throw an unawares Akio Oshiro into the backseat of the Falcon Devastator.

***

Earth's shadow is beginning to slowly seep onto the leading edge of the moon. This is the subtle indicator that the lunar eclipse has finally begun, and, as I imagine, when Alicia should be making her way up to Devil's Point and cracking open a bottle of some devilishly potent intoxicant, unwittingly lubing the stage for the most romantic fuckin' evening of her life. I can almost hear her calling out my name, Blik, Blik, Bli, Bl, B—echoing throughout the greater valley.

As I stand at the end of the miscellaneous items aisle, peering out through the window of the Puerto Rican liquor store, I can hardly believe how thoroughly unimpressed I am with the onset of this hallowed celestial event. If I didn't *know* it was happening, I certainly wouldn't *notice* it was happening.

Lunar eclipse? Exciting, it ain't.

I'm not zapped and tagged by a security drone on the way out so I can only assume that the store's auto-scan unit detected enough credits in my pathetic account to pay for the fresh pair of tube socks I've just made off with. I sit myself down on the warm concrete of the sidewalk and again reach for my boot buckles with that anxious longing that addicts must feel when they prep their needles with whatever it is they cherish most. But in my case it's just socks. Clean, dry, shrimp-slips crafted by the nimble digits of robots and powered by the energy generated from minerals siphoned from the lands of people who can't afford shoes. Bless them all, who suffer my needs.

I unbuckle my boots and wonder why it is that a liquor store would carry socks in the first place. Thank God they do—but why? How many requests did they get before they finally placed socks on the shelves? Do they have a suggestion box? Did it require a meeting? Did they have extra space or did something less lucrative than socks get bumped from the menu? What would socks out-sell at a liquor store?

Some hapless kid is staring at me like Oliver Twist at a taco stand and I'm seconds from punching him in the nuts. I wrench off a boot and peel off a sock, closing my eyes with a smile as the evening breeze whistles betwixt my toes. *Oh, heavenly respite, collect me!*

Off goes the other boot and then the other sock.

What the hell is this kid looking at? He's really getting on my nerves. I wiggle my toes and try to look tough.

"Children go missing all the time, kid, and nobody notices," I tell him, wondering if I look threatening enough while I rub my wrinkled feet. By his lack of expression, I don't think I fazed him, or he's perplexed by my actions, or he's trying to hypnotize me with his mind. But most likely he's trying to parse my personal profile from off the grid and he's now locked in the general response loop that's returned to a user's neural chip when trying to digitally transpond a pony or wombat or some other unplugged denizen like me. Good luck, kid. I'm a ghost. I've just walked another five miles in combat boots on a summer night, with wet socks that have been bunched up at my toes for hours. If I wanna massage my feet on the curb, I'm gonna massage my feet on the curb. And if he gets all teary-eyed and asks if I can spare some fresh socks, I'm gonna break his will in three.

"Are you Blik?" he asks, blinking his eyes rapidly to clear the infernal transmission in his neuro-chip.

Shit. He knows my name.

He must be an assassin or an agent of the grid selling subscriptions to the monthly feed. Either way, my best move would be to stab him in the thigh and run.

"How do you know my name?"

"My sister wants to know if you want a ride to Devil's Point. She's right over there," he says, pointing to a beat-up old car hovering next to the curb at the far end of the block.

My heart skips a few beats, realizing this pediatric pauper is *mi amore's* little brother.

I can just make out Alicia in the distant car, hunched over, fiddling with the dash, looking aloof as if she didn't just send her brother over to invite me into her incomplete life. She's probably digging about searching for just the right tune to play during the moment of our embrace when time slows to a crawl and her brownish-bluish-reddish tinted hair blows gracefully in the cinematic wind.

But what if she asks me why I'm sitting on the sidewalk rubbing my feet? Or does it matter? She stopped the car so she must truly be something special (or weirder) than I imagine. Whatever the case, I'm game if she is and she's just opened the opportune door for me to walk on through.

I slip on a fresh sock, pulling it up past my calf, and then I get the goose bumps. This is China White wrapped in bacon strips, main-lined through a garden hose. I slip on the next, then on with the boots, hopping up from the curb to meet my destiny, but the police cruiser that's just pulled next to Alicia's car alters my plans for the second time tonight, so I detour into the nearest alley and keep on walking.

First I'm sitting on the curb massaging my wrinkled shrimps, then I'm flaking on Alicia's invite. I might be losing points, but we won't be making sweet love if I'm locked-down for being a minor accomplice in a probable abduction, so I'll have to make it up to her when the heat dies down.

I turn back to see her little brother look over his shoulder, stopping to see that I've disappeared. Poor kid. I bet he had one simple task for the night, but now he won't get his alms.

Technically I didn't abduct Akio, but failing to alert the cops to a crime is a crime in itself, and biting the whistle to keep Akio out of the picture ... well, that's just so petty I'm almost ashamed. But love is a crazy beast, and good decisions make for a boring epitaph.

I sidestep through an unlocked door, making my way down a dimly lit bar past blue-haired old ladies, sipping green-tinted mint juleps. The din of patrons grows louder as I slide by the typical gathering of drunkards and late night lonely hearts, drifting through to the dining area where clicks of rowdy prep kids and unruly malefactors wreak havoc on tomorrow morning's cleaning crew. I seat myself at a window-side booth where there's a clear view of Alicia outside trying to sweet-talk her way out of a parking infraction that I am blithely responsible for. The police cruiser is positioned to the rear with its lights flashing that piercing red-n-blue strobe, but nobody in the Zone would give it a thought unless shots ring out or somebody takes off their pants.

I pull a simple black cube from my jacket pocket and place it on the table next to the un-cleared dishes of the diners that came before me. Some gracious bastard left a slice of crispy bacon for me to nibble on and I contemplate the perils of eating found-meat as I wash it down with a sip of somebody else's leftover cola. The sole waitress is occupied taking the orders from a party of revelers across the room, so now is as good a time as any to assess the device that I lifted from the suspicious-looking satchel in the trunk of Nance's Devastator. Anything worth kidnapping a man for is probably far too dangerous to leave in the hands of tuggers like Nance and Tim and I wouldn't want them to hurt themselves trying to parse it out, without the adult supervision of a parent or guardian. If anyone is going to get hurt doing something stupid, it's me. That's just the kind of friend I am.

It makes a faint beep that goes unnoticed as I turn it in my fingers trying to figure out which way is up, its black surface showing no visible seams or glyphs. Each touch generates a colorful glow that illuminates and fades beneath my fingertips. It looks innocuous enough, like a child's game, but so does a nuclear detonator or a fistful of warm plutonium. It's not till your kid's skin starts peeling off that you have second thoughts about rummaging through garbage bins for birthday presents or eating bacon off a stranger's plate. But maybe this is a toy. It isn't a stretch to think that Nance would exact a mortal revenge over a heated round of Teapots and Teddy Bears, but something tells me that this puzzle is more sinister ... and fun.

The waitress approaches and leans in to clear the dishes, glaring at me for seating myself at a table obviously sized for six.

I smile at her and say hello, still toying with the object in my hands, as she slows her task and turns her gaze to the device. I squeeze its sides, yank and pull, then shake it like a maraca until the colored lights intensify and increase in regularity. When I stop, the lights fade and so does my interest. I place it on the table and think about ordering pancakes.

"Try spinning it like a top," the waitress suggests, putting down the plates and wiping her hands like she's decided to stay a while. She seats herself across from me, putting her elbows on the table and her chin in her palms, fixating on the object with a curious grin.

I pivot the object on one corner and give it a good twist, sending it flying off—then under—the table.

The waitress gasps and retrieves it quick, looking to me with an anxious smile.

"May I?" she asks.

Before I can answer she snaps the device between her fingers setting it into a perfect rotation. The colors come alive and blur into one, pulling in my full attention. It emits a pleasant tone, hypnotic, almost like it's humming a tune.

I look to her with congratulations, but she is transfixed; frozen in a stare as the object slows and tumbles to a stop.

I'm about to laugh at her childlike fascination, but hold.

This lady isn't joking. She's as still as a statue and I realize the only sound I hear is the distant whirr of the kitchen fans. Looking about I see that everyone in this joint is frozen in place like a three-dimensional pictograph laced with the delicious smell of chicken-fried steak. I consider the object and sneak the last piece of leftover bacon, washing it down with what I hope is just a cup of coffee.

Yup, it's just coffee.

I take another swig to clear the bacon from my gums and turn to look outside.

Alicia is gone, but the cop is still there, standing by his cruiser and rigid as a board. The lights continue to flash. I hear the unmistakable crunch of a vehicle smashing into a wall and immediately know that some dumb hot-rodder like Nance must have disabled his car's auto-guidance assist thinking that there's something cool about the mathematical probability of human ineptitude. I bet he doesn't think he's so cool now. What a chump.

I take the object and spin it again hoping, halfheartedly to reverse the effects, but it just bounces off the table like before. I pick it up and try again, but bumble it over and over until I decide I lack the necessary motor-skills to get this tuggin' cube to twirl on end. These people might die because I spent my childhood playing with *myself* more than outside.

But first things first. If Alicia is still functioning she's going to need a little reassurance and a nice cuddle.

I dash outside and over to the nearest car, hovering in the street, it's auto-nav having slowed it to a stop. I pull the driver out and he goes from stiff to limp as I throw his body to the ground. Sorry, mister.

I jump inside and close the door. The dash lights illuminate the cabin in a soft, colorful glow. It's pretty posh, actually. Nice glossy, faux-wood paneling and leatherette upholstery. The indicator board is plainly visible, not overly-stimulating, and it seems that the designers really took their time placing the navigational and audio accoutrements. I push a button and a cup holder slides out of the door. Nice. The steering column is just the right height and protrudes to an appropriate distance from my shoulders to where my elbows have a comfortable bend while my hands grip the slip-free, finger-grooved steering wheel. All-in-all I think I would enjoy the ride if I knew how to start the engine of one of these floating pieces of crap, but alas, I don't. Long gone are the days of turning a key or jabbing it in the side with your spurs.

I spot another option and jump back out to the sidewalk, B-lining it for a frozen kid with a backpack in one hand and a MagSlide in the other.

I snake the floating plank of plastic death from his grasp and toss it to the ground, watching as it equilibrates on its magnetically induced cushion of air.

I hop on, push off, and regain consciousness a few minutes later with an even better plan in mind.

***

The walk up to Devil's Point was unusually pleasant so I took my sweet time but, noting the current position of the Earth's umbra, I have a few more minutes before the eclipse is total, and so far I'm utterly unimpressed. Sure, Alicia is probably scared and helpless wondering what's become of the world, but she'll be all the more ready to leap into my arms if I can time this thing to my advantage. I'm wearing a fresh pair of socks and everyone I passed is in a horrifying state of suspended animation. The Zone is quiet for the first time ever and I think I saw a raccoon. It's a dream come true and I'm going to revel in it first and worry about it much, much later.

My best guess is the obvious answer, that this little black device disrupts the neural chip implants welded to the brains of most, used to augment the gathering and processing of information. If this is true, then unplugged saps like me would be impervious to its influence due to the lack of hardware hardwired to the synapses of our noggins. But who knows what this device is truly intended for? You can kill a man with microwaves or just make a bag of popcorn. Not every sword has a double edge and rendering most of humanity in a catatonic state could just be an interesting side effect of a more benevolent intention. Nevertheless, the potential strategic global ramifications are staggering enough to keep me mildly interested for at least the next hour.

I can see the silhouettes of dozens of people sitting at the top of the hill as I come near, the crested moon before them giving the night sky a soft haze above the city lights. But no one moves, trapped like the rest in a queer hibernation.

Nestor and the gang sit in varying states of suspended revelry, staring at a spot where the moon used to be about an hour ago. They look like they were having really a good time without me. Bastards.

Footsteps disturb the grass somewhere in the distance and I turn to see Alicia, radiant in her signature red coat and lipstick, approaching up the hill at a hurried paced with a bottle in her hand. Unplugged, like me. She looks understandably worried by the unusual turn of events, her eyes big and watery. I ready myself for her warm embrace.

"What the hell, asshole?" she calls out, slipping a little and maneuvering for better footing while the bottle she's holding tips this way and that, splashing liquid onto her sleeve.

"Blik," I say softly, correcting her with a smile.

"Asshole!" she repeats, working for breath as she reaches the top. "My little brother was really upset that you just took off like that."

I look about with feigned concern.

"Where is the little fella?"

She stops within smooching distance and puts her free hand on my shoulder for balance, motioning loosely down the hill with the other.

"In the car, frozen like the rest of them," she says, righting herself as she meets my eyes with a saucy smile. "It's just you ... and me."

I'm certain that the right response is out there somewhere, floating about in the ethereal void, but I all can think to say is, "Please tell me you're not drunk."

"I'm not drunk," she replies. "Not yet."

Alicia holds on tight to my affectionate gaze, staring in my eyes with her exquisite feminine longing, and I can't help but think that she's taking this whole situation with remarkable poise when somebody hits me on the ear so hard I can hardly hear Alicia scream.

A mess of expletives coalesce in my head but never manage to clear my throat and I drop to my knees, the infernal ringing of head trauma blaring in my skull.

Someone kicks my shoulder hard, knocking me onto my back. I turn my head to the side opening my eyes and can barely make out the distinctive red-n-blue strobing lights of a hundred police drones flying toward this hill from several miles out, the noise of their sirens barely cutting through my haze.

I can feel a frantic hand patting at my sides and digging into my pockets when the form of Akio Oshiro comes into focus, hunched above me, holding a gun, and looking pretty pissed off.

"I never liked you, Blik," he reminds me, pulling the little black device from my jacket and standing just long enough to kick me in the ribs.

I'd forgotten how much it hurts to get my ass kicked.

Alicia yells, "Asshole!" (presumably at Akio this time) and I turn my head to see him pull her away by the arm. He has a small, curious, metallic device taped to the back of his neck.

They fumble through the crowd of hypnotized onlookers, knocking them over like pork dominos as they pass.

The low hum of police drones intensifies as they speed closer, silhouetted before the distant glow of the Zone sky.

The moon is barely visible now, with just a sliver of light cresting its side until that too fades away. And still, I am unimpressed.

Akio is fifty yards away by the time I manage to get to my feet, pulling Alicia across the ridge of the hill. I look about to find something to throw, my legs still wobbling from the blow to the head.

I pick up a stone and position it in my hand, trying to keep sight of Akio who is beyond the far side of the frozen revelers and moving quickly with Alicia struggling by his side. I throw it, trying not to lose my tenuous balance, and it goes high into the sky in a hopeless arc, landing far short of the intended target.

Cotton socks aren't cheap. Compared to a car or an off-world vacation, they're pretty cheap. But to someone who can't afford generic shampoo, cotton socks aren't cheap—and they're something I would never considering tossing out until my toes are exposed to daylight. So I pull one of my old, damp socks from my back pocket and pick up another stone, placing it at the midpoint and folding the sock over for a makeshift sling. I recall some historical precedence for this sort of maneuver, which gives me some hope as I swing the rock above my head with ever increasing velocity. I consider, however, that David didn't get bonked on the noggin before killing Goliath, and he certainly didn't do it with a wet sock.

My form is good and the release is snappy, sending the rock shooting out with impressive speed in completely the wrong direction. The problem with stone-age technology is that it sucks and a lot of dames in distress had to suffer the beast before anybody could sort that out.

But it does land with enough of a thud to draw Akio's attention, giving Alicia the opportunity to smash her bottle over his head.

Good girl. Goodbye, Akio. We'll need to find more alcohol.

I hobble toward her, carefully making my way through the crowd of living mannequins, the hilltop lit by the frenetic beams of hovering drones, circling above, examining the scene.

She walks toward me, smiling, fixing tangles and brushing some grass from her hair.

She stops close enough for me to feel her breath on my neck and the sensation is nearly euphoric. She takes my hand and places the little black device in my palm.

"Look," she says, turning her gaze to the sky.

The moon, once darkened by a penumbral shadow, is now a stunning blood-red, blanketed by the soft refracted light passing through the atmosphere of Earth. The lunar eclipse is in full salute and the only word to describe it is "captivating."

"Wow," we say in unison, as I slip my hand over hers.

We turn to each other again as the red-n-blue lights of the closing police drones scatter in all directions. Their spotlights converge and illuminate us in a brilliant white glow while Alicia's hair blows cinematically in a wind I can't even feel. She closes her eyes as I lean in to kiss her cherry-red lips.

Here come the fireworks. Here comes the bang.